THE UNINTENTIONAL ADVENTURES
OF THE
BLAND SISTERS

⊢⊢⊢ The Uncanny Express ⊢⊢⊢

THE UNCANN

by **Kara LaReau**

Illustrated by **Jen Hill**

AMULET BOOKS
NEW YORK

Library of Congress Cataloging-in-Publication Data
Names: LaReau, Kara, author. | Hill, Jen, 1975– illustrator.
Title: The Uncanny Express / Kara LaReau ; illustrated by Jen Hill.
Description: New York : Amulet Books, 2017. | Series: The unintentional adventures of the Bland Sisters ; book 2 | Summary: When their Aunt Shallot, aka Magique, Queen of Magic, goes missing on the Uncanny Express, Jaundice, Kale, and the famous detective Hugo Fromage seek to solve the mystery and rescue the magician.
Identifiers: LCCN 2016049054 | ISBN 9781419725685 (hardback)
Subjects: | CYAC: Sisters—Fiction. | Missing persons—Fiction. | Railroad trains—Fiction. | Humorous stories. | Mystery and detective stories. | BISAC: JUVENILE FICTION / Mysteries & Detective Stories. | JUVENILE FICTION / Fantasy & Magic. | JUVENILE FICTION / Family / Siblings.
Classification: LCC PZ7.L55813 Un 2017 | DDC [Fic]—dc23

ABRAMS The Art of Books
195 Broadway, New York, NY 10007
abramsbooks.com

For Pearl, who lived just long enough
to see me through this
—K.L.

THE UNINTENTIONAL CAST OF CHARACTERS

Jaundice & Kale

Frank Harold

Magique

Hugo Fromage

Countess Goudenoff

Vera Dreary

Cecily Springwell

Desmond Goode

Colonel McRobb

Kirk Hatchett

★ Tillie's Tip ★

TO CLEAN YOUR TOILET PROPERLY,
add ¼ cup chlorine bleach to the bowl
and let it stand before scrubbing.
Don't forget to flush!

Chapter One

It was a particularly uneventful afternoon in at least one house on the road to Dullsville. To say that it was particularly uneventful is saying a lot, as this house was occupied by none other than the Bland Sisters, Jaundice and Kale.

You might tell the Bland Sisters apart in several ways.

First, Jaundice prefers to dress in gray, while Kale favors brown.

Second, Kale wears her hair parted on the side, while Jaundice parts hers in the middle.

Third, Jaundice is left-handed while Kale is right-handed.

Fourth, Kale is seldom seen without her backpack, in which she currently carries *Tillie's Tips*, a worn little paperback featuring page after page of housekeeping advice, supplemented with helpful (if slightly dated) black-and-white illustrations. Kale came across this particular title at the Port Innastorm Library several weeks ago and has already renewed it twice. She finds *Tillie's Tips* incredibly helpful—and, of course, she finds comfort in knowing that there is someone out there who is more obsessed with cleaning than she is.

Fifth, Jaundice is known to wear a smock featuring an inordinate number of pockets. She tends to pop items in her pockets at random, providing herself with such treasures as a lone shoelace, two or three paper clips, a handful of clothespins, and a slightly damp kitchen sponge. Jaundice does not always remember to empty her pockets before her smock goes into the wash, much to the continued chagrin of Kale, who does the laundry.

Other than these few distinctions, the Bland Sisters are just about the same.

Jaundice and Kale pride themselves on their exacting routine. After breakfast (plain oatmeal with skim milk, a cup of weak, tepid tea on the side) they tend to their business of darning other people's socks, which takes the better part of the day. Each allows herself one ten-minute break, during which she eats a cheese sandwich on day-old bread (or hardtack biscuits, thanks to a recipe the Bland Sisters recently acquired) and drinks a glass of flat soda while gazing out the window, watching the grass grow.

The Bland Sisters look forward most to the evenings, when they entertain themselves by thinking of numbers divisible by three then staring at the wallpaper until they fall asleep. Not long ago, they enjoyed the nighttime ritual of reading a dictionary aloud to each other; since that dictionary left their possession, they have decided to broaden their horizons.

It should be mentioned that Jaundice and Kale have parents. Evidently, they are adventurers of some sort and send the Bland Sisters accounts of their travels whenever they can get to a mailbox. This is fine with Jaundice and Kale, as they much prefer reading about adventures to actually having them. And besides, they are sure their parents will return any day now. Certainly, one can only be away from the comforts and routines of home for so long.

In any event, not only was nothing happening to the Bland Sisters on this particular day, it seemed as if *less* than nothing was happening. Their business of darning other people's socks had been slow that week, so Jaundice and Kale had already finished mending the few they'd been given. The daily oatmeal and weak, tepid tea and cheese sandwiches and flat soda had been consumed, the grass-growing had been observed, and the Bland Sisters were several hours away from bedtime and its accompanying rituals. Nevertheless, they succeeded in passing the time; Jaundice found solace in tying knots in a piece of string (knots had become her new hobby, ever since the Bland Sisters had been tied up by their toes and nearly keelhauled by pirates), and Kale occupied herself with her favorite of all chores: cleaning the bathroom, which she accomplished with her implement of choice, an old toothbrush.

It was in the middle of scrubbing the inside of the toilet tank that Kale suddenly dropped the aforementioned toothbrush. Normally, this sort of mishap would cause her to cry out, as no one, not even a Bland Sister, wants to have to reach into the murky waters of a toilet tank to retrieve anything. But in this case, Kale was too preoccupied to make any sort of noise.

"Jaundice?" she finally called out to her sister.

"Yes, Kale?" Jaundice replied, working on a particularly difficult knot.

"I'm having a Feeling," Kale announced.

Jaundice sighed, looking up at the ceiling. Her sister was always having Feelings. It was very

trying. Not so long ago, Kale had a Feeling, and the Bland Sisters were subsequently kidnapped by the aforementioned pirates, forced into menial labor, and stranded (if only temporarily) on a deserted island. Sometimes, Jaundice wished her sister would keep her Feelings to herself.

"Did you hear me?" Kale asked, emerging from the bathroom.

"I heard you," said Jaundice. "So what kind of Feeling are we talking about this time?"

"I'm having a Feeling something's about to happen," said Kale.

"And what happened after you started having this Feeling?" Jaundice asked.

Kale thought for a moment. "I dropped my toothbrush into the toilet tank," she said.

"A toothbrush in the toilet tank," said Jaundice. "That *is* quite a happening."

"I don't think that's it," said Kale, closing her eyes.

"And why not?" asked Jaundice.

"Because I'm still having the Feeling," said Kale.

"Is the toothbrush still in the toilet tank?" asked Jaundice. Kale nodded.

"Well, there you go," said her sister. "You'd better go fish it out."

"What a relief," said Kale, rolling up one sleeve. "I was really starting to think something more serious was going to happen. You know, like last time. With the pirates."

"Perish the thought," said Jaundice, getting up from the couch. "I'm going to go out to the mailbox."

"But today's my turn to get the mail," said Kale.

"Given where your hands have been all afternoon," her sister said, "I think you should sit this one out."

"Good idea," said Kale. Jaundice was almost always right.

IF YOU'RE EXPECTING GUESTS,
spend at least a week cleaning
and preparing. And stay calm.
No one likes a stressed hostess!

Chapter Two

The Bland Sisters' mailbox was a metal box nailed to a wooden pole. A red flag on the box would be turned up by the neighborhood postal carrier, Miss Penny Post, if mail had been delivered. Jaundice and Kale had learned this the hard way; recently, they discovered that several years of correspondence had accumulated in the mailbox, as neither of them had been checking it regularly.

Today, the red flag was up. Jaundice felt a twinge of excitement. She had signed up for a subscription to a magazine called *Nuts for Knots* and was very much looking forward to her first issue. Unfortunately, upon opening the mailbox, Jaundice beheld an envelope far too small and thin to hold any periodical.

"We've got a letter," Jaundice announced as she returned to her place on the couch. She ripped open the envelope with one finger, careful not to give herself a paper cut.

"Is it from our parents?" asked Kale, emerging from the bathroom. Jaundice passed the letter to her sister so she could read it for herself.

Darling daughters,

Fabulous news—your Aunt Shallot is coming to town! She'll be looking for you at the Dullsville depot on Saturday just before noon; we hope you might help her with her bags and with anything else she might need. We're sure you'll recognize her immediately, but just in case, she says she'll be wearing one of her trademark hats, and she now has gray hair and wears glasses.

Have fun!

Yours,

Mom and Dad

"A visitor? Staying here? What shall we do?" said Kale, wringing her hands.

"I suppose we'll have to send for a fresh sundries basket," Jaundice said. The Bland Sisters received a regular delivery from the Dullsville Grocery, a basket which included bread, cheese, soda, sock-darning thread, and other necessities.

"But where will she sleep?" asked Kale. "She can't sleep on the couch. Where will we do our sock darning? And where will we watch the grass grow?"

"Maybe she should sleep in one of the rooms upstairs," suggested Jaundice.

The Bland Sisters rarely ventured into the upstairs of their house, where their parents had slept and worked. To conserve heat, Jaundice and Kale kept the door leading upstairs closed and locked.

"I don't think we should allow guests up there," said Kale. "It's private."

"It's not like anyone is using it. And besides, it's just Aunt Shallot. She's family," said Jaundice. She reread their parents' letter, noting the date. "She's coming on Saturday. What's today?"

"Friday," said Kale, after a moment of thought.

Jaundice stood up. "That's tomorrow. Next time I see Miss Penny Post, I'm going to have a word with her. At this rate, I'll be as old as Aunt Shallot before I see my first issue of *Nuts for Knots*."

"If you need me, I'll be cleaning. Starting with the bathroom," Kale announced, retreating to the toilet, which she decided needed rescrubbing.

WASH YOUR SHEETS ONCE A WEEK —
we spend one-third of our lives in bed,
leaving behind sweat, body oils, dead
skin cells, and drool!

Chapter Three

That afternoon, Jaundice went to the garage to determine what mode of transportation they might use to pick up Aunt Shallot, and Kale continued with her cleaning.

When their parents left so suddenly on their errand of an unspecified nature so many years ago, they had taken the car. The garage was drafty and empty, with the exception of several stacks of flowerpots, an old sack of fertilizer, a bicycle with a flat tire, a rusty wheelbarrow, and a red wagon.

Right away, the bicycle was out, since neither Bland Sister knew how to ride one, let alone change a tire. The wheelbarrow seemed a bit clumsy to navigate and a bit

10

inappropriate for picking up a guest from the train station, unless that guest happened to be of the botanical variety. It would have to be the red wagon, Jaundice decided, assessing it warily. Had it ever been used? She couldn't remember. The wagon was in nearly new shape, though it was not very large. Jaundice hoped that Aunt Shallot was on the smaller side.

While Jaundice wrangled the transportation, Kale finally finished rescrubbing the bathroom and set to work getting a bed ready. Unfortunately, the upstairs rooms were filled with boxes and trunks of their parents' things, which the Bland Sisters had packed away long ago. Even though Jaundice and Kale were sure their mother and father would return any day, it was much easier to keep the house clean without so many *things* lying around.

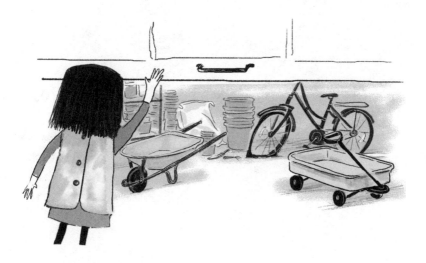

Kale managed to locate their parents' bed, though it was covered with boxes of books and documents and maps. Carefully, she piled all the boxes against the wall, next to the suitcases filled with their parents' clothes. After she was done, she assessed the bed. The sheets would definitely have to be washed, she decided.

"Sister?" Jaundice called from downstairs.

"Up here," replied Kale, as she heard her sister climbing the stairs.

"What are you doing?" asked Jaundice.

At this point, Jaundice had entered the room to find Kale stretched out on their parents' bed. One of the pillows was over her face.

"Just seeing if the bed is comfortable enough for Aunt Shallot," she said, her voice slightly muffled. "Also, I'm smelling this pillow."

"What does it smell like?" Jaundice asked.

"Like our mother, I think," said Kale. She handed the pillow to Jaundice, who stretched out next to her sister on the bed and gave it a whiff.

"Hmm," said Jaundice. "You might be right."

She took another pillow from behind her head and held it out to Kale. They sniffed it together.

"Is this what our father smelled like?" Kale wondered.

Jaundice shrugged. "I don't remember."

"There goes that ache again," Kale said, clutching her chest.

"I feel it, too," said Jaundice.

For a little while now, both sisters had been experiencing the same sensation, in the area where their hearts were beating. The ache was slightly painful, but also strangely comforting, which made it difficult to diagnose via their copy of the *Dullsville Hospital Home Health Handbook*.

"Well, even if we don't remember much about our parents, at least we know neither of them has an unpleasant odor. That's something," said Kale. "So, do you think Aunt Shallot is our mother's sister or our father's?"

"It's hard to say," said Jaundice. "What do you remember about her?"

Kale looked into the middle distance, as she usually did when she was thinking.

"Nothing," she said, finally.

"Me neither," said Jaundice.

"They say she'll be wearing one of her 'trademark hats,'" Kale said. "Maybe we can look out for someone with unusual headwear."

"Good idea," said Jaundice, yawning.

Kale yawned back. "I really should start washing these sheets. But this bed feels so . . . cozy."

"Maybe we should lie here for another minute or two, just

to make sure it's truly comfortable enough for Aunt Shallot," Jaundice suggested.

"It's the very least we can do as hosts," Kale said, closing her eyes.

Within moments, the Bland Sisters were asleep. Kale dreamed that the house was a mess, but all she had to clean it with was her toilet-cleaning toothbrush. She did what she could to clear away her parents' maps and books and clothes and souvenirs, but there was just too much stuff.

Jaundice dreamed that a phone was ringing. She went to the kitchen phone to answer it, but there was no one on the other end. Still, somewhere in the house, the ringing continued.

Ring-ring! Ring-ring!

It sounded particularly urgent. And it seemed close, as if it were right under Jaundice's nose.

✶ Tillie's Tip ✶

IF YOU SHOULD LEAVE THE HOUSE FOR ANY LENGTH OF TIME,
make sure to empty your trash before you go.
No one wants to return home to the smell of garbage!

Chapter Four

Hours later, when the Bland Sisters awoke in their parents' bed, they were hugging each other.

"Jaundice," Kale whispered. "Jaundice."

"What?"

"I think we fell asleep," Kale said, looking at the clock. "It's already morning."

Jaundice sat up. She reparted her hair in the middle. She looked around. Even though the shades were drawn, the sun was visible behind them. Both sisters squinted.

"Did you hear a phone ringing last night?" Jaundice asked. "I think I dreamed it."

 "I didn't hear anything. I dreamed I was trying to clean the whole house, using only a toothbrush," said Kale. "Which reminds me, I should really wash these sheets."

Jaundice looked at the clock. "Let's eat first. I'm not myself until after I've had my plain oatmeal and weak, tepid tea."

Soon, a leisurely breakfast was enjoyed, and Kale was already on her second load of laundry. Jaundice stretched and sighed.

"That's better," she said. "You know, I've forgotten my dream altogether."

"Me, too. Though I feel like we're forgetting something else," Kale said.

"Well, the house is clean. We'll have fresh food once the sundry basket arrives. And the red wagon is ready to take to the train station—" Jaundice said, suddenly remembering.

"The train station!" said Kale. It dawned on her, too.

"We need to pick up Aunt Shallot!" the Bland Sisters said at the same time.

The Bland Sisters had never been to the Dullsville Train Station, but there was really no time to take in the sights. By the time they arrived, it was almost noon, when Aunt Shallot's train was due to arrive.

"I don't like train stations," Kale decided. "There's too much hustle. Not to mention bustle."

"And it's too loud. I can barely hear myself think," said Jaundice, who was still angry at herself for forgetting the red wagon.

"If only we had more information," Kale said.

"Or any information, really," said Jaundice.

That's when both sisters' eyes came to rest on a sign hanging over a desk in the center of the terminal. Fortunately, the sign read INFORMATION.

"We're looking for our aunt," Kale said to the man sitting behind the desk. "We're supposed to pick her up here just before noon."

"Quite a few trains arrive and depart around that time," the man said. "On which train is she due to arrive?"

"We don't know," said Jaundice.

"Well, where is she coming from?" the man asked.

"We don't know that, either," said Kale.

The man raised his eyebrows. "Well," he said. "I suppose we could make an announcement over the loudspeaker, to let her know you're both here. What's your aunt's name?"

"Shallot," the sisters said.

"Is that her first name or her last name?"

Jaundice and Kale looked at each other. Then they looked at the man at the information desk and shrugged.

The man sighed. He grabbed his microphone.

"AUNT SHALLOT . . . AUNT SHALLOT . . . PAGING AUNT SHALLOT . . . YOUR NIECES ARE WAITING FOR YOU AT THE INFORMATION DESK."

"Thank you," said Jaundice.

"You're welcome. Good luck," said the man. Almost immediately, he looked past the Bland Sisters to his next customer and barked, "Next!"

Jaundice and Kale sat down on a bench close to the Information Desk.

"Do you think we'll be waiting long?" asked Kale.

"Who knows?" said Jaundice.

"Well, let's do something to pass the time," Kale said. "We don't have any socks with us to darn. Shall we do our numbers?"

"All right, then," said Jaundice. "Three."

"Ooh . . . six!" said Kale. It really was fun, thinking of numbers divisible by three.

"Nine," said Jaundice.

"Oh, thank goodness!" a voice said.

Coming toward the Bland Sisters was a woman dressed all in black. She wore a long coat and had a big scarf looped around her face, with a floppy hat on top. And she wore very big sunglasses. She seemed to be struggling with her bag, a very large purple satchel.

"She's wearing a hat," Kale whispered to Jaundice.

"And glasses," Jaundice whispered to Kale.

"Is that you, Aunt–?" Kale asked.

"We don't have a lot of time," Aunt Shallot said, tossing her satchel to Jaundice. "I hope you two are fast runners."

The Bland Sisters had never run anywhere together, on any occasion. But now seemed as good a time as any to try.

"This would have been much easier if I'd remembered the wagon," Jaundice managed, between running, carrying the purple satchel, and trying to follow Aunt Shallot.

"Why are we running *toward* the trains instead of away from them?" Kale asked.

"Less talking, more running," Aunt Shallot advised. Eventually, she navigated them to Track Nine. Both sisters noted that this was a number divisible by three; somehow, this seemed like a good omen.

The train on Track Nine was called the Uncanny Express. Aunt Shallot passed the first car, marked BAGGAGE, and ducked into the second car, marked PASSENGER, while Jaundice and Kale followed behind, as quickly as they could. They might have been good at running if the purple satchel Jaundice was carrying weren't so heavy. Kale tried to carry the bag at one end, but in her attempt to help her sister, she ended up tripping over a ruddy-faced man with a briefcase and a walking stick.

"Watch it, missy!" he growled.

"Sorry," said Kale.

The Bland Sisters stepped aside as an older woman in a mink stole with a small fluffy dog was followed by a younger woman in a tweedy coat and hat.

"We're almost there, Countess," the younger woman said cheerfully. "We're in compartment four."

"I don't see why we have to rub elbows with the hoi polloi," the older woman said, clutching her pearls as she looked down her long nose at the Bland Sisters. Her little dog bared its tiny teeth and growled at Jaundice and Kale.

"Ah," Aunt Shallot said, noting all the numbered compartments. "Here we are. Number one. How apropos."

The compartment was paneled in wood and featured a large window against the far wall, framed by facing bench seats covered in green leather, with a little fold-down table in between. On the table was a single red carnation in a bud vase. Luggage racks hung over the bench seats on each side, and above a button on the wall, a plaque read PRESS FOR SERVICE.

A red envelope leaned against the bud vase. Aunt Shallot opened it and gasped. Quickly, she closed the envelope and tucked it into her coat.

"Did you forget something here?" Kale asked.

"I don't believe so. Now that I've found you ladies, I have everything I need," Aunt Shallot said, clapping her hands.

25

"All right, then," Jaundice said, attempting to catch her breath. "We should all be getting on now."

"Yes, we should," said Aunt Shallot.

"Well, we'll have to get off the train," said Kale.

"Eventually, yes," said Aunt Shallot. She sat down on one of the seats and opened her satchel. She took out a pack of playing cards and began shuffling them, cutting them, and shuffling them again.

The sound of a piercing whistle made Jaundice and Kale jump.

"All aboard!" a voice said outside.

"We have to get off this train. Now," Jaundice said.

"Whatever for?" Aunt Shallot asked. "Did *you* forget something, dear?"

"I think you've forgotten that you're supposed to come with us, Aunt Shallot," Kale said.

The woman laughed. "'Aunt Shallot'? Sounds like a real fuddy-duddy," she said.

"I'm having a Feeling," said Kale.

Jaundice was, too. It was the feeling of the ground moving beneath her feet. The train was moving, and the Bland Sisters were on it, whether they liked it or not.

Chapter Five

"Pick a card," the woman said, fanning them out to Kale.

"Two of hearts," said Kale, holding it up for Jaundice to see.

"Excellent," said the woman. "Now stick it back in the fan."

Kale did as she was told. The woman collapsed the fan, then shuffled the deck several times, the cards flowing from one hand to the other like water. She cut the cards, shuffled one last time, then held the deck in one hand and flipped the top card over.

"Two of hearts," said Kale. "Whoa."

"So, who are you?" Jaundice asked. The Bland Sisters had

many rules for themselves, including Never Open the Door to Strangers. Getting on trains with strangers—let alone engaging in card tricks with them—was on another level entirely.

The woman removed her sunglasses, unbuttoned her long black coat, and stood up. Underneath, she wore a purple robe covered in silver lightning bolts.

"I am . . . MAGIQUE!" she announced with the wave of a hand.

When she took off her hat and head wrap, the Bland Sisters could see that Magique's hair was silver, too.

"Magique?" Kale said.

"I know, you're overwhelmed to be in my presence. I get that a lot," Magique said. "But you'll get used to assisting the Queen of Magic, eventually."

"I think there's been a misunderstanding," Jaundice said, finally.

"Oh? I was told there would be two young female assistants waiting for me," Magique said.

"Well, we're not them," said Jaundice.

"Then whyever did you get on the train with me?" said Magique.

"We . . . thought you were someone else," Kale tried to explain. "Someone who is probably at the Information Desk right now, waiting for us."

"Tickets, please!" the conductor said, poking his head in.

Magique pulled out a pile of papers from her satchel and handed them to him. The conductor stamped them one, two, three times.

"You had tickets for us?" Kale said.

"Of course," said Magique. "That was the arrangement. The two young ladies were to travel with me to the Uncanny Valley, for my big show."

"My name is Mr. Harold, should you need anything," the conductor told them, tipping his hat.

Just then, a young couple appeared outside the compartment. The woman was beautiful, with perfectly curled blond hair and green eyes and bright pink lipstick. A handsome man with dark, slicked-back hair was pulling her by the hand.

"Can I help you?" Mr. Harold asked the couple.

"Just making our way to compartment number three, old chap," said the young man. He smiled, revealing a set of pearly white, perfectly straight teeth. "I know the way."

"You know *everything*, darling," said the young woman, giggling as the young man led her off.

Mr. Harold sighed. "Have a nice day," he said to Magique and the Bland Sisters, then moved on to the next compartment.

"So, who made this arrangement with you?" Jaundice asked. She looked at Kale. The Bland Sisters already knew the answer.

"Your parents," Magique said, reaching into her satchel again and producing a letter from a very worn envelope, addressed with all-too-familiar handwriting. She showed it to Jaundice and Kale. It said:

Dearest Magique,

We hear you're looking for a new assistant. Might we suggest two—our daughters, Jaundice and Kale? They're very smart and resourceful, and while they don't have experience with magic, they are well versed in the art of escape, having just eluded kidnapping by pirates. They should be at the Dullsville Train Station just before your noon train, waiting to meet you.

Yours from hither and yon,

The Blands

"'Kidnapping by pirates'? That's quite a résumé at your age," noted Magique.

"Well, that's true," said Jaundice.

"Why did they tell us her name was Aunt Shallot when her name is Magique?" Kale whispered to her sister.

"They tricked us with the whole Aunt Shallot story to get us on this train," Jaundice explained. "Our parents are trying to make us have another adventure."

"Don't they remember how they almost got us killed with the last adventure, with the pirates?" Kale wondered.

"We're not interested in being magician's assistants," Jaundice informed the magician. "We're getting off at the next stop. When is the next stop, anyway?"

"Well, this is the Uncanny *Express*, after all," Magique said. "The next stop will be the Uncanny Valley. Is there nothing I can do to convince you two to stay on? I have a big performance planned, and I'll need all the help I can get to pull it off."

"We run our own business, back at home," Jaundice explained. "So we're needed there right away."

"When the socks pile up, things can get messy," Kale added.

"That is a shame," Magique said, shaking her head. "Well, let's at least enjoy ourselves while we're all here together, shall we? Why don't we have lunch in the dining car, and I can fill you in on my show. If you're lucky, you might even learn about the big surprise I have planned. In a few hours, we'll arrive at the Uncanny Valley station, and I can send you both back to Dullsville."

"Lunch does sound good," Kale said, nudging her sister. After they'd spent some time without food on the pirate ship, the Bland Sisters learned to eat whenever they could.

"As long as they have cheese sandwiches," said Jaundice.

SOAK YOUR LINENS IN A SOLUTION
of aspirin and hot water—
they'll brighten like magic!

Chapter Six

Jaundice and Kale had never eaten lunch in such a fancy dining room, let alone a dining room on a train. As the landscape of Dullsville zoomed by, Kale admired the white tablecloths and shiny silverware while Jaundice scrutinized the menu.

"How do they keep their linens so *white?*" said Kale, consulting *Tillie's Tips* for possibilities.

"I don't see any cheese sandwiches," Jaundice noted, flipping the menu over.

"Leave the ordering to me," said Magique. When the waiter arrived, she announced, "Three croque madames and three glasses of lemonade."

Jaundice tugged on the waiter's sleeve as he turned to go. "We'd prefer soda, if you have it," she said. "The flatter, the better."

"It's so nice having traveling companions again," said Magique. "I've been on my own since I fired Albertine. She just didn't cut the mustard as a magician's assistant. Although she does possess certain unassailable qualities."

"Like what?" asked Kale.

"She's my daughter," said Magique. "Her grandfather— my father, Albertus Magnus—went by the name of Professor Magic. He was a world-class performer and an author."

Magique reached into her satchel and pulled out a book. She handed it to Kale.

"*Professor Magic's Rules of Illusion*," Kale read across the cover.

"I was his onstage assistant. Until he attempted his escape from the Inescapable Water Tank of Death. As it turned out, his greatest illusion was his downfall," Magique said, sighing.

"We're sorry for your loss," Jaundice said. "Drowning must be awful." The Bland Sisters were tied up and nearly keelhauled by their pirate

kidnappers not so very long ago. Jaundice still shuddered at their almost watery fate.

"No. His greatest illusion was *literally* his downfall. He fell as he climbed up the ladder into the tank," Magique explained. "Tumbled right into the string section of the orchestra."

"Well, no one deserves to die with any kind of violence," said Jaundice.

"Or *violins*," Kale added helpfully.

"He wasn't an easy father to love," the magician admitted. "Even though I was always the one who loved magic, he only wanted to teach my brother the business."

"Why wouldn't he teach you?" asked Jaundice.

"My father thought magic wasn't for girls," the magician explained. "Unfortunately for him, my brother had other plans, and none of the other up-and-comers was good enough to be his protégé. So my father allowed me onstage eventually, but only as his assistant. Every night, he sawed me in half, and levitated me high above the stage, and plucked coins from my ears, but I was never allowed to perform the effects myself. Instead, I learned and practiced all the techniques from his book in secret."

"I'd never be able keep the things I love secret," Jaundice said. "Tying knots at night would be awful. You really need the right lighting."

"If I didn't have the freedom to vacuum, I don't know what I'd do," admitted Kale.

"After my father died, *I* didn't know what to do," admitted Magique. "I had myself and Albertine to feed, and the only skill I had was magic. Eventually, I remembered the one thing my father did willingly teach me: The show must go on."

Magique took a coin out of her pocket and laid it on the table. She tapped the shoulder of someone dining at the next table, a mousy young woman wearing a tweedy coat and hat.

"Excuse me," said the magician. "Might I borrow your hat, just for a moment?"

"I—I suppose so," she said, handing it over. The woman dining with her was the one with the fur stole and the pearls and the white fluffy dog. She sighed.

"Don't encourage that woman, Vera," she said.

"Sorry, m'lady," the tweedy woman said, bowing her head.

"I'll have it back to you in just a moment," said Magique. She turned to Jaundice. "Heads or tails?"

"Tails, I guess," said Jaundice.

The magician spun the coin, then placed the hat over it. When she lifted the hat, the coin was tails.

"Do it again," Jaundice said. "Heads this time."

Again, Magique spun the coin, then placed the hat over it. When she lifted the hat, the coin was heads.

"Do it a third time, and I might actually be impressed," said a man in a bow tie two tables over.

The magician looked over at him and smiled. Again, she spun the coin, and covered it with the hat.

"You call it this time, Mr. Hatchett," she said.

"Heads," he said.

When Magique lifted the hat, the coin was tails.

"Aha," the man said. He was standing over Magique's shoulder now, and he looked very pleased with himself.

"Aw," said Kale. "Too bad. It was a really good trick, up to now."

"Wait," said Magique, turning the hat over and looking into it. "I think there's something in here . . ."

She reached in, then pulled out her hand and opened it. Laying on her palm was the man's bow tie. The man turned red as he felt around his neck, where his tie used to be.

"I think this is yours," she said, handing it over. Scowling, the man refastened the tie around his neck and retreated back to his table, where he and the gentleman with the walking stick began grumbling to each other. Magique returned the hat to the tweedy woman, who examined it closely before putting it back on her head.

"Whoa," said Jaundice.

"You sure showed him," said Kale.

"I hope so," said the magician. "It's taken me a long time

to regain my confidence. When I was set to debut at the Dullsville Music Hall, six months ago, I was nervous as all get-out. But Albertine was there for me. She said, 'Mom, you were always meant to be a great magician. Let's really show 'em.'"

"And did you?" asked Kale.

"I did," said Magique. "I levitated Albertine and sawed her in half. I did card tricks, rope tricks, and rabbit tricks. The audience seemed to enjoy it, until my mind-reading act."

"You read minds?" Jaundice said.

"Well, I tried," said Magique. "Just as I was in the middle of my reading, people in the audience started walking out. Once that happened, everyone else turned on me. They started booing. They even started throwing things. I still have a tomato stain on my robe, right here."

She extended her robe sleeve to Kale, who scrutinized it, then referred to *Tillie's Tips*. "We can get that out with a little laundry detergent and white vinegar," she said.

"When the tomatoes started flying, I took it as my cue to leave the stage," Magique continued. "But I didn't stop there—I started running. I ran all the way back to my house, up to my room, where I shut the door and threw myself on my bed and started crying. I cried for three days. And then, I stopped."

"Did you run out of tissues?" Jaundice asked.

"No," said Magique. "I ran out of figs."

The Bland Sisters looked at each other.

"Albertine was bringing me a fresh box of tissues when she said, 'Mom, you always taught me not to give a fig what other people think. You shouldn't give a fig, either.' From that moment on, I ran out of figs to give. I blew my nose, dried my eyes, and started making a plan."

"We love plans," said Kale.

"Well, this is the mother of all plans," said Magique. "This time, my act is even bigger, even more astonishing than it was before! And it all starts with the very thing the audience hated so much the last time: mind reading. Would you like to see a little bit of it?"

"As long as we can keep eating," Jaundice said, taking another bite of her croque madame. Once she scraped off the fried egg on top and removed the ham inside, it almost tasted like a cheese sandwich from home.

"First, empty your pockets," said Magique.

Jaundice did as she was told. It took some time, as she had many pockets in her smock, and she was always filling them with this and that. Today, she was carrying:

- ✦ **Two long pieces of string, not yet knotted**
- ✦ **A plastic bag, which had at one time contained the bread for the Bland Sisters' cheese sandwiches**

◆   A pen and a little notebook, in which Jaundice kept track
of the accounting for their sock-darning business

◆   A paperweight in the shape of a beetle

Magique put her fingers on either side of her head and
began rubbing her temples. "I am looking through the
Mind's Eye—the mind is our most powerful tool. If we use it
often and well, it will tell us many things and show us many
secrets."

The magician picked up Jaundice's pieces of string. She
held them between her palms.

"You've been in a real bind before," Magique said.

"That's . . . true," Jaundice said, looking at her sister.
When they were kidnapped by pirates, Jaundice and Kale
were once tied with ropes . . . around their big toes. This was
especially traumatic for Jaundice, whose toes had always been
sensitive. Since then, she'd become fixated on learning how to
tie and untie knots.

Magique held the plastic bag. "You prefer when things are
contained."

"Right again," said Jaundice.

Magique flipped through the accounting notebook. "You
run a tight ship," she noted.

"When it comes to our finances and/or pirates," said
Jaundice.

"And this," said Magique, holding the paperweight and

looking at Jaundice intently. "This possesses a singular weight. Something about it speaks to you."

"Our parents brought it back from one of their travels," Jaundice explained.

"How do you do that?" Kale asked. "Did you really read Jaundice's mind?"

"I could tell you," Magique said, leaning in. "But first, you'd have to take the Magician's Oath. Raise your left hands."

The Bland Sisters did as they were told. They repeated the following words after Magique.

✦ Magician's Oath ✦

I promise to uphold the tradition of illusion.

I will never perform any effect without first practicing until I can perform it well enough to maintain the illusion of magic.

I will never divulge magical secrets to a non-magician, unless that person swears to uphold the oath in turn.

I will extend nothing but respect and goodwill to my fellow magicians, for as long as I might wave my wand.

"Can I interest you ladies in anything?" Mr. Harold asked, wheeling over a little courtesy cart. "Newspaper, candy, gum, breath mints?"

"Do you have any hand sanitizer?" asked Kale. If she'd

known she'd be traveling, she would have brought her own bottle from home, per *Tillie's Tips*.

"I'm afraid not," said Mr. Harold.

Magique studied the selections and chose a box of Good & Plenty. The purple candy box matched her robes perfectly. "One of my favorites," she said, handing Mr. Harold some money. After he was on his way to the next table, she opened the box and held it out to Jaundice.

"Thanks, but we don't really like candy," she said.

"It's just so . . . *sweet*," Kale said, wincing at the thought of the one time their parents made them try it.

"Suit yourself," said the magician, tucking the box into her robe sleeve.

The Bland Sisters leaned in. "So, what's the secret of mind reading?" Jaundice asked.

"Well," said Magique, taking a long drink of lemonade. "The secret is that it's not really 'mind reading' at all. It's really all about guesswork and deduction and knowing how to read people. In my debut act six months ago, I assessed my audience, then I said general things, like, 'a man with a limp is hiding something,' and 'two young people in love are deceiving each other,' and 'a woman has committed a grave crime against her husband.' Then I waited to see if my readings registered with anyone."

"And had they?" asked Jaundice.

"Well, that's when people started getting up and leaving," noted Magique. "And then the tomatoes started flying."

"I'm sorry your 'mind reading' was a failure," Kale said.

"Oh, I have learned quite a bit from my mistakes," the magician said. She stood up and raised her arms and wiggled her fingers. "In fact, my mind now reaches out—to seek further connection!"

"I think I've lost my appetite," said the old woman at the next table. Her little dog growled in agreement.

"There is so much angry energy here . . ." Magique said, putting her hands on either side of her head. "In fact, I sense a crime will soon be committed, *on this very train!*"

The pretty blond woman with the green eyes stood up. "I sense a headache coming on," she said. Her handsome companion led her out of the dining car.

"Um," said Kale. "Maybe we should do this back in your compartment, where it's quieter."

45

"And safer," said Jaundice. "If you're right about that crime thing."

"But there are many more minds to read here," said Magique, gesturing around the room. "I sense many interesting stories—and many *juicy secrets!*"

The man with the walking stick called Mr. Harold over and grumbled something to him. They both glared in Magique's direction.

"Excuse me," said Mr. Harold, approaching the table. "I've been asked to tell you to quiet down. People would like to eat without distraction."

"If you continue with these shenanigans, there will be *consequences,*" the man with the walking stick warned, his face redder than ever.

"My magic will not be silenced!" shouted Magique. "Now that the Mind's Eye has opened, its secrets will be heard!"

"Well, they won't be heard on this train," Mr. Harold said, taking Magique by the arm. "Let's get you back to your compartment, madam."

Magique did not go quietly. She shouted on about her magic and the Mind's Eye and its secrets waiting to be revealed all the way back to her compartment. Jaundice and Kale followed until the man with the bow tie stopped them.

"Are you a part of Magique's 'act'?" he asked.

"We're just . . . passing through," Kale said.

"He's the one Magique talked to earlier," Jaundice whispered to her sister.

Kale nodded. "He didn't seem to like her very much," she said.

"How do you know Magique?" Jaundice asked the man.

"I'm Kirk Hatchett," he explained, twirling his pen around his fingers. "Entertainment reporter for the *Dullsville Mentioner*."

"We almost always have the *Mentioner* in our house," Jaundice said.

"It's come in handy on more than a few occasions," Kale added.

The *Dullsville Mentioner* was the local paper. Though Jaundice and Kale were not keen on actually reading the news, the grocer sometimes used old issues to wrap items in their weekly sundries basket, and per *Tillie's Tips*, Kale recycled the paper and used it to wash the windows. It really did help to minimize streaking.

"I'll be writing about Magique's comeback performance," Mr. Hatchett continued. "Though 'comeback disaster' is more like it, considering what her performance was like last year."

"You were there?" Jaundice asked.

"I was," said Mr. Hatchett, wrinkling his nose. "I'll give you girls a bit of advice: Stay away from that woman. She has no business being onstage. The only 'hit' she's going to have is the sound of the audience's tomatoes when they make contact. Actually, that's a pretty good line. I'm going to use it for my review."

The journalist scribbled something in his reporter's notebook.

"But you haven't even seen her new act," Kale reminded him.

"I've been in this business longer than you two have been alive," Mr. Hackett said. "Nothing surprises me anymore." He twirled his pen again and was on his way.

"Do you think he's right?" Kale asked her sister.

"I hope not," said Jaundice. "For Magique's sake."

Back in her compartment, the Queen of Magic looked royally exhausted. Yet, she was smiling.

"Well, that was fun, wasn't it?" she said.

"Was it?" asked Kale. Fun for her was cleaning, or removing a set-in stain, or finding new uses for steel wool, according to *Tillie's Tips*.

"It didn't seem like it went very well," noted Jaundice. "With Mr. Harold throwing you out and all."

"Oh, I think it went perfectly well. Sometimes the goal isn't applause. It's *attention*," Magique noted. She opened her satchel and took out her playing cards, along with several scarves of various colors, a stack of three brass cups, three red balls, and a birdcage. "Now, I must prepare for my performance. Just come get me when it's teatime, would you?"

With that, the magician closed her eyes and started shuffling again. The Bland Sisters looked at each other.

"I think this is her way of telling us to shuffle off," said Jaundice.

The Bland Sisters surveyed their own compartment. It seemed bare, without any luggage or magical paraphernalia like Magique's. Of course, they liked it that way.

"What shall we do to pass the time, then?" asked Jaundice.

"We can look out the window," suggested Kale. "And take in the countryside."

The Bland Sisters tried this for several long minutes.

"The sun is, as ever, very bright," noted Jaundice, shading her eyes.

"I've never seen so many trees," said Kale. "They're so leafy, and green, aren't they?"

"Too green, I'd say," said Jaundice.

"With the train moving so fast, it's hard to watch the grass grow," Kale said.

Both sisters sighed and pulled the curtains. Kale leaned back in her seat and remembered she was still wearing her backpack.

"I can read to us from *Tillie's Tips!*" she suggested.

"And I can get back to my knots," said Jaundice. She pulled out one of her strings and started practicing.

Eagerly, Kale pulled out her book. "Oh, wait."

Instead of *Tillie's Tips*, she was holding *Professor Magic's Rules of Illusion*.

"Somehow, our books got mixed up," Kale said.

"Well, you'll have to wait until later to switch them back. We don't want to disturb Magique," Jaundice said.

"I'll need Tillie back right away. She's due on Monday, and I want to renew her again," Kale said. "Plus, I was just getting to the chapter on dust. It covers a lot of ground."

"Do you still want to read?" Jaundice asked.

"I guess I could try," said Kale. She opened up the book and began.

Though it wasn't as practical a read as *Tillie's Tips*, *Professor Magic's Rules of Illusion* really was very informative; each chapter began with a bit of advice for young magicians, and it was beautifully illustrated to show how each illusion was achieved. Unfortunately, this was not enough to maintain the Bland Sisters' interest, as Jaundice was soon snoring, and Kale was asleep with the open book resting on her face.

Again, Kale dreamed that she was clearing away the clutter. Only this time, it was clear that someone was buried underneath it all and crying for help.

"Hold on, I'm doing my best!" she kept shouting, though there was now a thick layer of dust over everything.

Again, Jaunice dreamed that a phone was ringing, and that it seemed to be right under her nose.

Ring-ring! Ring-ring!

"Wait. Maybe *I* have the phone," she thought. She checked all her smock pockets.

No phone.

Ring-ring! Ring-ring!

It seemed more urgent than ever. And it seemed as if it would never stop.

⟜ Professor Magic's Rules of Illusion ⟞

The closest thing to feeling real magic
is performing for people and helping them
to experience the impossible.

⊞⊞⊞⊞⊞⊞⊞⊞⊞ Chapter Seven ⊞⊞⊞⊞⊞⊞⊞⊞⊞

D *ING! DING! DING! DING!*
A bell rang at exactly four o'clock, waking Jaundice and Kale.

Jaundice groaned. "Will that phone ever stop ringing?"
she said.

"I don't think that was a phone. It was some kind of
bell," Kale said wearily. She felt exhausted from all the dream
cleaning. And just who was buried beneath all that clutter and
dust? she wondered.

"Do you think that bell means it's teatime?" Jaundice
asked. She stood up, relieved that the dream ringing had
stopped. At least, for now.

"It's a bit late for tea," Kale noted. "It seems so dark."

"That's because you have a book on your face," Jaundice noted.

Kale removed *Professor Magic* and looked around.

"Ah, that's better," she said. "Shall we get Magique?"

It turned out the magician was nowhere to be found. Her compartment was empty, and it was a mess; playing cards and scarves and cups and balls were scattered everywhere.

"I can't find my book," Kale said, sifting through the clutter. "And this is when I'd really need *Tillie's Tips*."

Jaundice sniffed the air. "Do you smell something . . . burning?"

They looked around. On the little table against the window was the box of Good & Plenty, next to one of the luncheon plates from the dining car. On the luncheon plate was a red envelope and a partially burned piece of newspaper. The paper was still smoking.

"Fire! Fire!" Kale yelled. She ran from one end of the compartment to the other, waving her arms.

Jaundice took the carnation out of the bud vase and poured the water from the vase over the smoking paper. It fizzled out immediately.

"Whew," Kale said, wiping her brow. Between this and the dash through the Dullsville train station, she'd had enough exercise for a while.

"Why do you think Magique was burning that newspaper?" Jaundice asked. "And why do you think she left so quickly?"

"Maybe she heard the bell and got excited about teatime," Kale suggested. "I bet she's already in there, waiting for us."

The Bland Sisters stepped over the clutter and made their way to the dining car. Some of the other travelers were already in there, enjoying their tea.

Mr. Harold approached. "I'm afraid children aren't allowed in here without a chaperone," he explained.

"But that's just it," said Kale. "We can't *find* our chaperone."

"I'm sure she just stepped out, to the restroom, perhaps," Mr. Harold suggested. "Why don't you go back to her compartment and wait for her?"

"But, her compartment is a mess, and she left something burning—" Jaundice began to explain. But Mr. Harold was being called over by the gentleman with the walking stick, who demanded extra raspberry jam for his toast.

"What do we do now?" asked Kale.

"*Excusez-moi, mademoiselles.* Perhaps I can be of service?" a man asked in a thick accent. He was small and round and

bald, with a very shiny black mustache, an impeccable suit, and a gray homburg hat. He observed Jaundice and Kale through funny wire spectacles without earpieces that were perched on his beaky nose.

"We're not ordering anything," Jaundice explained, waving him away. "We're looking for our friend."

"And I am not a waiter," the man said. "I am HUGO FROMAGE, THE GREAT DETECTIVE!"

"Great detective?" Kale said.

"At your service," the man said, executing a dramatic bow. "No doubt you have heard of me and the crimes I have solved. The Mysterious Affair at Kyle's? Thirteen at Brunch? The Murder of Roger Adenoid?"

The Bland Sisters could only shake their heads.

"No matter," said the detective, with a flourish of his gloved hand. "I am willing to serve any client, no matter how uneducated or uninformed."

"But we don't have any money here, and we only have just a little at home, which we've earned by sock darning," Kale explained.

"Maybe Magique can pay you, once you find her," Jaundice suggested. "I bet she has money. After all, her father was a famous magician. And he had a book published; she must be rich."

"Very well," said Hugo Fromage. "First, let us search her compartment."

"We already have," said Kale.

"But not with HUGO FROMAGE, THE GREAT DETECTIVE," Hugo Fromage reminded them. "There is nothing I do not notice or remember. As we go, please tell me everything you know and recall about your traveling companion—what she said, what she wore, what her luggage looked like . . . and how she seemed."

"How she seemed?" asked Jaundice.

"*Oui*," said the master detective. "The victim's temperament can be very telling."

"She seemed eager for her next performance," Kale recalled.

"She said she had something really big planned," added Jaundice. "Something 'astonishing.'"

As the Bland Sisters recounted their experiences with Magique, Hugo Fromage listened intently, until—

SCREECH!

The train jolted. Jaundice, Kale, and Hugo Fromage bumped into one another. Teacups and spoons went clattering to the floor. Someone in the dining room gasped. The woman in the tweedy coat nearly dropped the pitcher of cream she was holding. The lights flickered, then went off, then went on again.

"What's going on?" Mr. Hatchett asked Mr. Harold as the conductor ran by.

"There's an abandoned truck near the tracks," Mr. Harold quickly explained. "A Fluff-O truck. The driver must have gone for help when the back doors came unlocked—barrels are overturned everywhere, and the Uncanny Express is now stuck."

"What's Fluff-O?" Kale asked.

"I believe it is marshmallow crème," explained Hugo Fromage. "Among other things, it is used as a spread, commonly accompanied by peanut butter in a sandwich known as a 'fluffernutter.'"

"That sounds . . . terrible," said Jaundice. Kale grimaced in agreement.

"It also sounds messy," said Mr. Hatchett. "How long is it going to take to clean up?"

"I'm not sure yet," said Mr. Harold. "I'll update you whenever I can."

The Bland Sisters leaned outside, where they could see the truck next to the tracks, its back doors open, surrounded by broken Fluff-O barrels. The marshmallow crème clung to the tracks and the wheels of the Uncanny Express like heavy, sticky snow.

"Follow me, *mademoiselles*," Hugo Fromage said. "With this delay of the train, we now have more time to get to the bottom of our mystery."

Slowly, meticulously, the detective inspected Magique's train compartment. He looked underneath and behind the seats, just as the Bland Sisters had, but he also knocked against all the walls, stomped on the floor, and tried pulling up the carpet. He scrutinized each  and every scarf, ball, cup, and playing card. Then he turned to the box of candy and the dish of burned paper.

"You say there was a fire in here?" he asked.

The Bland Sisters nodded. Hugo Fromage pulled out a handkerchief and wrapped the candy box, the red envelope, and the burned, wet scraps inside.

"What are you doing?" asked Kale.

"Collecting evidence," explained the great detective, looking around the room. "Anything out of the ordinary, great or small, must be considered with suspicion."

His eyes fell on something stuck in the door hinge. Gently, he opened the door and dislodged it.

"What is it?" asked Jaundice.

"A torn piece of fabric," said Hugo Fromage, holding it up.

"It's purple," said Kale. "Like Magique's robe."

"And it has a stain on it. A red stain," said Jaundice. "She showed that to us earlier, when she was telling us about how her last audience threw tomatoes at her."

"I know all about stains, thanks to *Tillie's Tips*," said Kale, squinting. "And that isn't the same one she showed me before."

"How right you are, *mademoiselle*," said the great detective. "This stain is fresh, and it is not from tomatoes. It is darker, and redder, perhaps from something else. Something . . . like blood!"

The Bland Sisters shivered.

"I must collect this evidence. If only I had brought along another handkerchief," said Hugo Fromage.

"You can use this one," said Jaundice, pulling a handkerchief from one of her smock pockets. "I found it just outside, after we first realized Magique was missing."

"*Mademoiselle*, I cannot use this to collect evidence. For this *is* evidence," the great detective explained. The handkerchief was crisp and white, with green embroidery around the edges, and the letter *H* embroidered in one corner, surrounded by flowers.

"It's pretty," noted Kale. "I wonder who it belongs to?"

"The *H* is not for *Hugo*, that is certain. But I will be holding on to it for the foreseeable future," said the great detective.

Jaundice dug into another smock pocket and produced the plastic baggie. "How about this, then?"

"Perfection," said Hugo Fromage. Once the evidence was properly collected, he clapped his hands. "Now, shall we take a look at the rest of the train?"

The great detective and the Bland Sisters walked up and down the three cars of the Uncanny Express, including the passenger car, the dining car, and finally, the luggage car.

"This looks promising," the great detective said, gesturing to a large purple cabinet. Jaundice read the label hanging from one of its knobs.

"It belongs to Magique!" she exclaimed. "And it's supposed to be delivered to the Uncanny Valley Hippodrome. I bet it's for her show."

"I have heard of this type of apparatus before. In the world of magic, I believe it is known as a *disappearing cabinet*," Hugo

Fromage explained, running his gloved hand over its gilded trim.

"I bet she's inside!" exclaimed Kale.

But when she flung open the doors, the cabinet was empty. Hugo Fromage rummaged around the cabinet's interior, just to be sure. Then he stood for a moment, thinking. Finally, he looked up at Jaundice and Kale.

"There is definitely something missing," said the great detective.

"Other than Magique?" asked Kale.

"Indeed," said Hugo Fromage. "In your account of your magician friend, you said she carries a purple satchel. There is no satchel here, as you see."

"And it wasn't back in her compartment," noted Jaundice. "What does that mean?"

"There are three possibilities, I think," said the master detective. "The first is that your employer has left the train."

"You mean, she jumped off?" Jaundice said.

"*Précisément*," said Hugo Fromage.

Kale looked out the window. "But the train was going so

fast. Even if she didn't take a heavy satchel with her, jumping off a speeding train wouldn't be a good idea."

"I did say there were three possibilities," the master detective said.

"What are the other two?" asked Jaundice.

"The second is that your employer may be hiding."

"But we've already searched the train, and we couldn't find her anywhere," said Kale.

"Unless she's in one of these, which really wouldn't be a good idea," said Jaundice, assessing the various stacks of luggage. Nothing seemed big enough to hold a full-grown magician.

"Well," said Hugo Fromage. "There may indeed be a third possibility."

"Which is . . . ?" asked Kale.

The master detective raised his perfectly waxed eyebrows. "Foul play, of course."

"What is 'foul play'?" asked Jaundice.

"It means 'danger,' *mademoiselle*," explained Hugo Fromage. "It means that someone on this train has made your magician disappear—against her will. And it means we have a mystery on our hands."

"We're not big fans of mysteries," said Jaundice. "Unless they're in books."

Indeed, the Bland Sisters had very recently started reading

a series of books about two intrepid brothers named Keith and Joe Nubbins, aka the Nubbins Twins. The second book in the series, *The Mystery of the Secret of the Clock Under the Stairs in the House on Cabin Island*, looked very promising.

"What do we do now?" asked Kale.

"Unfortunately for the perpetrator, Hugo Fromage is on the case!" said the master detective, jabbing his gloved finger into the air. He turned on his heel and waddled away. Over his shoulder, he shouted, "Follow me to the dining car!"

Quickly and quietly, Hugo Fromage informed Mr. Harold and the other passengers of the situation: Magique was missing, and the Uncanny Valley Police should be notified. In the meantime, he announced, he would be conducting an investigation.

"Where do we even start?" asked Jaundice.

"We start with a list and a map," said the great detective, handing Kale a clipboard. "This list is called the *passenger manifest*. Every person who bought a ticket for this journey should be accounted for, and this diagram of the train compartments should show us where they should be situated, *oui*?"

"Um . . . *oui*," said Kale. She looked at the manifest. "This is a lot of people."

"And a lot of compartments," said Jaundice, looking at the diagram.

"Then we must work quickly," Hugo Fromage said, pulling out two chairs from one of the dining tables. "Please, be seated, *mademoiselles*. The first suspect is due to arrive at any moment."

"What are we supposed to do?" asked Kale.

"Why, assist me, of course," said the great detective.

THE UNCANNY EXPRESS

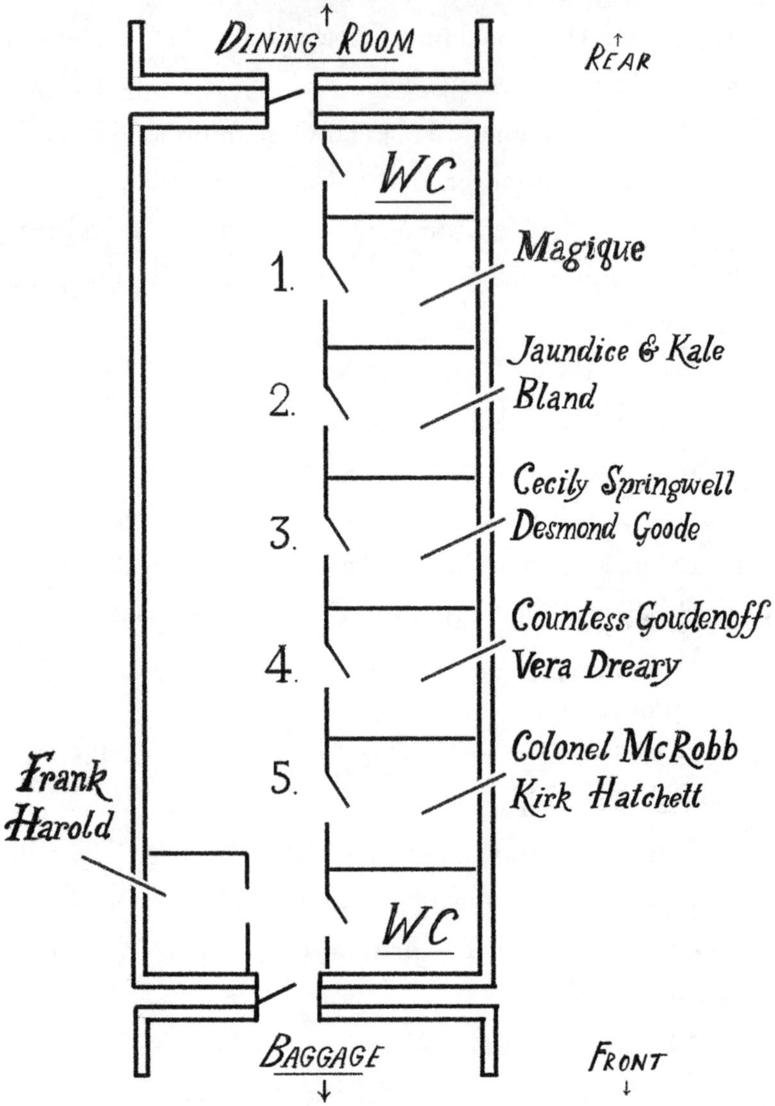

DINING ROOM

REAR

WC

1. Magique

2. Jaundice & Kale
Bland

3. Cecily Springwell
Desmond Goode

4. Countess Goudenoff
Vera Dreary

5. Colonel McRobb
Kirk Hatchett

Frank
Harold

WC

BAGGAGE

FRONT

66

"The last person we were supposed to assist was Magique, and look how that turned out," Jaundice reminded him. "I'm not sure we're the best people for the job."

"You already have the best person for the job, and that is Hugo Fromage," explained Hugo Fromage. "I am intelligent, clever, and experienced in all things, particularly crime solving. But I find it is helpful to have an entirely different perspective, which I am sure you two can provide."

"Well, when you put it that way, how can we say no?" said Kale.

"Just remember, *mademoiselles*, the key to being a good detective is to be *observant*," said the great detective.

"'Observant'?" repeated Kale. On these occasions, she sorely missed her dictionary.

"It means we must pay close attention to everyone and everything," Hugo Fromage explained.

"Sorry, what did you say?" asked Jaundice, still considering the clipboard.

The great detective sighed.

"As ever," he muttered, "Hugo Fromage will rise to the challenge."

☛ **Professor Magic's Rules of Illusion** ☚
It's normal to be nervous before a performance:
It shows you care about doing a good job.

⊞⊞⊞⊞⊞⊞⊞⊞⊞⊞⊞⊞⊞ Chapter Eight ⊞⊞⊞⊞⊞⊞⊞⊞⊞⊞⊞⊞⊞

T he first suspect, as it turned out, was none other than the conductor himself, Frank Harold. He served Hugo Fromage and the Bland Sisters tea before he sat down to be questioned.

Jaundice and Kale sighed as they took their first sips. To their delight, the tea was perfectly weak and tepid.

"Can you tell me, *monsieur*, how long you have been employed by the Uncanny Express?" the great detective asked.

"Just about six months now, I think," Mr. Harold said.

"Can I borrow your pen and accounting notebook?" Kale whispered to her sister.

"Okay," said Jaundice, retrieving them from one of her smock pockets. "Just don't mess with my tallies. We still have a sock-darning business to maintain."

"Don't worry. I'll be doing a different kind of accounting," said Kale. "If Monsieur Fromage expects us to be observant, I figure it might help to take notes—like that reporter, Mr. Hatchett."

"And you were here, in the dining car, to witness Mademoiselle Magique's performance?" the great detective asked the conductor.

"I was, but I wasn't really paying attention," Mr. Harold admitted. "I was on my way back from delivering some tea to Countess Goudenoff. She insisted on having it in her compartment. And then Colonel McRobb stopped me to ask for more raspberry jam. He's the gentleman with the walking stick."

"When I was getting on the train, I tripped over his walking stick, and he called me 'missy,'" Kale remembered. "And not in a nice way."

"Can you tell me, have you ever come across Mademoiselle Magique before?"

"Never," the conductor said.

"What about the other passengers on the train?" Hugo Fromage asked. "Are you . . . *familiar* with any of them?"

"I am familiar with all of them," the conductor said, clearing his throat. "That's my *job*."

The great detective sipped his tea. He pursed his lips.

"Of course," he said. "But, are you familiar with any of the passengers outside of your job? Have you ever seen them anywhere else before this particular journey?"

"I . . . don't believe so," said Mr. Harold. "Then again, there may be some passengers who have traveled before. But I'm not aware of any right now, off the top of my head."

A long silence followed. Jaundice and Kale looked at each other. Mr. Harold began to fidget in his seat.

"I really must be going," the conductor said. "I have work to do."

"Very well, then. That will be all. For now," Hugo Fromage said.

The conductor rose from his chair and crossed the room.

"Oh! One more thing," the great detective said. He reached into the plastic bag and produced the handkerchief. "Is this yours?"

The conductor turned around. When he saw the handkerchief, he looked surprised.

"Certainly not," he said, finally.

"I ask, only because of the letter *H* embroidered here," Hugo Fromage said. "And your last name being Harold."

"Well, that's obviously a woman's handkerchief, and I am clearly not a woman," the conductor said.

"*Clearly,*" said Hugo Fromage, smiling. "Good day, Mr. Harold, and thank you for your assistance."

"You call *that* assistance?" Jaundice said, after the conductor had left the dining car.

"What did *you* observe, *mademoiselles?*" Hugo Fromage asked.

"Well, he seems like a hard worker," said Jaundice.

"And he makes perfectly tepid tea," offered Kale, making sure to write this down in the notebook. "But he didn't tell us anything useful at all."

"*Au contraire, ma chère.* Sometimes a 'tell' is not about what one says. Sometimes it is about how one *reacts,*" the great detective said. He pushed away his teacup and saucer and dabbed at his mustache with his napkin. "Unlike this tea, I'd say things are just heating up."

☞ Professor Magic's Rules of Illusion ☜

To truly amaze your audience,
you must tell small lies.

Chapter Nine

W hat's all this, then?" Colonel McRobb asked, limping over to the table where Monsieur Fromage and the Bland Sisters sat. As he took a seat across from them, he placed his briefcase on his lap.

"We are hoping you might be able to assist us," Hugo Fromage explained, "as we investigate the disappearance of Mademoiselle Magique."

"Ugh, that flaky trickster?" said the colonel, crossing his arms. His face flushed scarlet.

"Be that as it may," said the great detective, "we have reason to believe she had enemies. Enemies who may be on this very train. Had you ever seen Mademoiselle Magique before?"

"I don't go in for that magical balderdash," said the colonel. "I am only interested in *reality*, sir."

"Yes, you must have faced many harsh realities in your time at war. Your injury, how did it happen, if I might ask?" the great detective asked, gesturing to the colonel's walking stick.

"I jumped out of an airplane during a rescue mission," the colonel explained, puffing out his chest. "My parachute didn't open, so I landed in a tree. I broke my leg in the fall."

"Ouch," noted Jaundice. Her toes were particularly sensitive, though she preferred to avoid trauma to any and all extremities.

"After I untangled myself, I crawled nearly a mile in the pitch dark until I found a cave, where I created a splint for my leg out of branches. I remained there for days, eating nothing but nuts and berries and small woodland creatures," the colonel continued. "When I was finally able, I snuck into the enemy's camp and rescued my comrades."

"Most unfortunate," Hugo Fromage said, shaking his head.

"Especially for the small woodland creatures," noted Kale.

"It was most *fortunate*," the colonel said, "that the enemy never took me alive. And that I was able to save my fellow soldiers."

"I, too, served in the military. Though I did not exhibit such grand acts of heroism during my tenure," the great detective admitted. "Might I ask why you are traveling on the Uncanny Express this afternoon?"

"I'm out promoting my memoir," Colonel McRobb explained. He opened his briefcase just wide enough to pull out a book, which he placed on the table.

Kale picked it up. "*True Hero: One Man's Fall to Glory*," she said, reading the title and subtitle emblazoned across the front cover.

"It's been number one on the *Dullsville Mentioner*'s bestseller list for the past six months," the colonel said, smirking. "My publisher has me doing an event at Uncanny Valley Books tomorrow. In the meantime, I'm being

interviewed for a feature in the *Mentioner*, by their entertainment reporter."

"I congratulate you on your success, Colonel. And I thank you for your assistance," said Hugo Fromage, pulling out the handkerchief. "By the way, does this look familiar to you?"

Colonel McRobb scoffed. "I'd never carry around such a flouncy thing. Or associate with anyone who would. Now, if you'll excuse me, I have an interview to finish."

As Hugo Fromage watched the colonel limp away, Jaundice said, "I guess we can cross him off the list of suspects."

"You think so, *mademoiselle*?" the great detective asked. "So, you observed nothing of interest about the colonel?"

"He mentioned being interviewed by an entertainment reporter. That must be Kirk Hatchett," Jaundice remembered. "The one with the bow tie who always twirls his pen."

"And he seems very protective of his briefcase full of books," surmised Kale, writing down this keen observation. She turned to her sister. "Maybe we can get a copy of his memoir. His story sounds *unbelievable*."

"Indeed," said the great detective.

☛ Professor Magic's Rules of Illusion ☜
Never repeat an effect. If you do,
you give the audience another chance to figure it out.

Chapter Ten

I really don't see the need for this," Countess Goudenoff said, pursing her crimson lips. She stroked her tiny white dog as she sat before the Bland Sisters and the great detective. "Aren't magicians *supposed* to disappear?"

"It seems this magician may have had enemies, Madame Countess," Hugo Fromage explained. "Can you tell me your reason for traveling on the Uncanny Express today?"

"I am en route to my summer home. It's just beyond the Uncanny Valley, in The Cramptons," the countess explained.

"The Cramptons?" Kale repeated, her pen poised. "Is that with a C or a *K*?"

"With a C, *mademoiselle*. It is a seaside resort," explained the great detective.

"An *exclusive* seaside resort," corrected the countess.

"I am sure it is beautiful this time of year," said Hugo Fromage. "And what were you doing just prior to teatime? I do not think I saw you in the dining car with the other passengers."

"I was in my compartment, waiting for Vera, my maid," the countess explained. "The conductor had left us the tea, but he'd included a pitcher of milk, and I'd *expressly* asked for cream. I sent Vera to the dining car to fetch some for me. Then the train jolted when it stopped to avoid whatever fell on the tracks. That's when it happened."

"What happened?" asked Kale.

"The tea spilled, all over my Chrysanthemum," the countess explained.

"Pardon?" the great detective asked.

"Chrysanthemum, my shih tzu," said Countess Goudenoff, gesturing at the dog in her lap, who regarded them all listlessly. "If the tea had actually been hot, she would have been terribly burned. Thankfully, this train has awful service."

"I am so glad to hear it," said the great detective. "Might I ask, have you ever come in contact with Mademoiselle Magique before?"

"I do not associate with *magicians*," the countess said coldly.

"I am sure you do not," said Hugo Fromage. He pulled out the handkerchief. "And does this look familiar to you?"

Countess Goudenoff narrowed her eyes. "Why would it? Goudenoff starts with a G, after all."

"What is your first name, if I might ask?" inquired the great detective.

"It is Ima," said the countess.

"*Ima Goudenoff?*" Jaundice said.

"You are," said Kale, patting her sister's hand.

"Ima begins with an *I*, and not an *H*," said the great detective, squinting at the handkerchief.

"You *are* sharp-witted," said the countess, looking down her nose at Hugo Fromage.

He bowed his head. "You have been of great assistance, Madame Countess."

Jaundice rolled her eyes. "She didn't tell us anything helpful," she whispered to her sister. "All we know is that she likes dogs. And vacations in 'The Cramptons.' And cream in her tea."

"And ordering people around," Kale said, adding this to her notes. "Though, I guess, when you're that rich, you expect everything to be done your way."

"You may return to your compartment, Madame Countess, where I will make sure the conductor brings you some fresh tea. With cream," said the great detective.

The countess sniffed. "Just make sure it's hot this time," she said. When she rose, Chrysanthemum jumped out of her arms. The dog teetered awkwardly over to Hugo Fromage.

"She doesn't seem very good at walking," noted Kale.

"Or keeping her eyes open," whispered Jaundice.

"Chrysanthemum, come to mommykins," Countess

Goudenoff said, clapping her hands and making kissy noises. But the dog did not move. It looked up at Hugo Fromage with half-lidded eyes.

"I think she likes me," the great detective said, reaching down to pet Chrysanthemum—just as she vomited all over his patent leather shoes.

"Naughty doggie!" scolded the countess.

"Of course," said Hugo Fromage, with a sniff, "I could be mistaken."

☛ Professor Magic's Rules of Illusion ☚
A gaff is an object that looks normal
but does something tricky.

⊞⊞⊞⊞⊞⊞⊞⊞⊞⊞⊞ Chapter Eleven ⊞⊞⊞⊞⊞⊞⊞⊞⊞⊞⊞

Vera Dreary wrung her tweedy hat in her hands.

"I di'n't do nuffin'," she said. "I was just fetchin' the cream for my mistress, for her tea."

"Your mistress, Countess Goudenoff, had asked for cream?" the great detective asked. Recalling the chapter on Pet Messes from *Tillie's Tips*, Kale had managed to clean Chrysanthemum's "contribution" from Hugo Fromage's shoes and was now buffing them with a dinner napkin.

"I'm sure I heard her say milk the first time, so that's what I ordered from the conductor. But then she insisted she said cream. Until then, we was havin' a nice moment there in the

compartment. She'd
even invited me to pour
a cup for myself. Then
she saw the milk, and it
was all off. When I got
back with the cream,
I told her about the
accident, and that there
was a detective on the
train. That's when she
stood up and spilled the
tea."

"I see," said Hugo Fromage.
"And how long have you been working for the countess?"

"Oh, about five years now, since me mum passed," the maid
said, hanging her head. "She'd worked as a maid, too, for the
countess and her husband, Count Goudenoff, rest his soul."

"When did the Count die?" asked Kale.

At this, the maid put her head in her hands and began
sobbing.

"Almost a year ago, his heart just gave out. He was such a
good man, he was," Vera said. "Not that *she* ever took notice.
But he was kind to me. He hired me, after me mum passed.
Even gave me this right before he died—I carry it with me
everywhere."

At this, the maid produced a framed photo of Count Goudenoff.

"He looks like a nice man," Jaundice offered.

"Oh, he was. The nicest. 'I'll always look after you, Vera,' he said. Them's the last words he ever spoke to me," said the maid. And then she collapsed in sobs altogether.

"There, there, *mademoiselle*," said the great detective, handing Vera a handkerchief. Just as she was about to dab her eyes with it, he asked, "Does this belong to your mistress?"

"But the countess already told us—" Kale said, referring to her notes, before Hugo Fromage waved her off.

"Please respond," he said to the maid, who was inspecting the handkerchief.

"It's not hers," Vera said, finally. "I iron all of her linens, so I would have noticed it. And besides—she wouldn't be caught dead wearing green."

"Plus, there's no *H* in her name," added Jaundice.

"Oh, is that an *H*?" said Vera, squinting at the embroidery. "I thought it was an *N*. You know, as in—"

"*Nut?*" Hugo Fromage suggested.

"That's right," said the maid, shifting in her seat.

"This is all very helpful to know," said the great detective.

"One other thing I should mention," said Vera. "When I opened the door to get the cream for the countess, I could swear I heard a woman's voice in the hallway say something like 'She's going to ruin everything.' But when I stepped out, the only one there was Mr. Harold. He was just standing out there with the empty tea tray, looking very shifty indeed."

"Hmm . . . this is curious," said Hugo Fromage. Kale agreed, making sure to write it all down.

"Will that be all, then?" asked Vera. "I must be getting back to my mistress. She'll be wanting something by now, no doubt."

"If I might ask one more question: Have you ever previously seen the magician, Mademoiselle Magique, or anyone else on this train?" asked Hugo Fromage.

"Oh, I've only ever been on a train one other time, when I came to take up my service with the count and countess," Vera explained, wringing her hat again. "Since then, I've only ever gone where my mistress tells me to. Can I go now?"

"Very well," said the great detective, as the maid scurried out.

"That bit about her hearing the woman's voice in the corridor was helpful," noted Jaundice. "Though she said she only saw Mr. Harold standing out there."

"She seems so anxious, the poor thing. It's too bad she's stuck working for such a mean lady for the rest of her life," said Kale.

"It is true. One wishes her fate might be different," said the great detective.

"It doesn't seem like she had anything to do with Magique's disappearance, either," said Jaundice.

"Let us not be too hasty," said Hugo Fromage. "Even those

who seem most innocent have a way of bringing the truth to light."

"Excuse me, sir?" Mr. Harold said, rushing into the dining car. "You are needed in compartment four. Evidently another crime has been committed."

"*Sacrebleu!*" exclaimed Hugo Fromage. He leaped to his feet and followed the conductor, the Bland Sisters trailing behind him.

It turned out compartment four belonged to the countess and Vera Dreary. Vera was wringing her hat again, and the countess was looking particularly annoyed.

"Someone has stolen my garnet ring!" the countess exclaimed.

"And when do you believe this theft took place?" asked the great detective.

"When I was with *you people*, being questioned about this ridiculous magician," the countess said. Then she glared at Vera. "And *you* left the compartment unattended!"

"I had to—use the facilities," Vera explained sheepishly. "I was only gone for a few moments, I swear it!"

"You were not wearing the ring, then?" Hugo Fromage asked.

"It is a large ring, so I can only wear it for so long before it fatigues my delicate fingers," the countess explained.

Jaundice gave Kale a nudge. Countess Goudenoff had gnarled fingers tipped with long, dark red nails. They seemed more talon-like than "delicate."

"Eventually, I took it off, and I gave it to Vera to put in my train case," the countess continued, glaring at her maid again.

"I put in in the train case, just as you asked, m'lady," Vera insisted. "I di'n't do nuffin'!"

"You said she seemed anxious," Jaundice whispered to her sister. "I wonder if *she* stole the ring."

"You think so?" said Kale.

"How else is she going to afford a better life for herself?" Jaundice noted.

Kale nodded. Jaundice was almost always right.

The countess turned to Hugo Fromage. "I purchased that ring right before my husband's tragic passing, so it is priceless to me in *every way*," she explained.

The great detective looked around the room then picked up the train case and inspected it. He set it back on the seat next to Countess Goudenoff and bowed his head.

"Madame Countess," he said. "One way or another, I promise we will get to the bottom of this."

"'We?'" said Jaundice.

"As my assistants, I expect you to help me with whatever investigations I am conducting," Hugo Fromage explained. "And now, we return to the dining car, tout de suite."

"But now you have *two* crimes to solve," Kale said. She considered her notes, which already seemed overwhelming.

"And you only have one brain," noted Jaundice.

"Ah, yes, *mademoiselles*, but there are three of us," said the great detective, waddling ahead of them to the dining car. "So the crimes, they are woefully outnumbered."

Misdirection is the art of controlling
where and what the audience focuses on.
It is in your gestures, what you say,
and where you look.

Chapter Twelve

M y goodness, are you *really* a detective?" Cecily Springwell
asked, widening her already-wide green eyes.

"I am not merely a detective, *mademoiselle*. I am HUGO
FROMAGE, THE GREAT DETECTIVE," said Hugo
Fromage, the great detective. "Surely you have heard of me."

"Not really," the young woman admitted, to his
disappointment. "Though I don't go in for all that cops-and-
robbers stuff. Desmond is the one who keeps up with all the
crimes in the papers. He seems rather obsessed with them,
really."

"Is Desmond the man you're with?" asked Jaundice.

"He is. Isn't he *dreamy*?" said Cecily.

"He does have very nice teeth," noted Kale. "They look like the tiles in our bathroom after I've given them a good scrubbing."

"We met six months ago, on this very train!" Cecily said. "I was on my way to the millinery in the Uncanny Valley to have some hats made, and he was on a business trip. He travels quite often, in his line of work."

"And what is that, his line of work?" asked Hugo Fromage.

The young woman scratched her head. "It's something to do with some import-export blah-blah-blah," she explained. "I don't have a head for business, or much of anything else. It's a good thing I'm easy on the eyes, as my fiancé says!"

"Desmond is your fiancé?" Kale asked.

"He is my everything, as I tell him," Cecily said, putting both perfectly manicured hands over her heart. "I don't have any family, since both my parents are gone and I haven't any other relatives. It's so nice to know that I'll have someone to share Fernwood with me."

"We don't have family, either," Kale explained. "Well, except for our parents, though we haven't seen them in years. And our aunt Shallot."

"But our parents made up Aunt Shallot, to get us to the train station, remember?" Jaundice said.

"Oh," said Kale. "So we're never going to meet her?"

Jaundice sighed. As she attempted to spell things out for Kale, the great detective returned his attentions to Cecily.

"So what is Fernwood, *mademoiselle?*" he asked Miss Springwell.

"That's the name of my parents' estate. Well, it's my estate now, since I inherited it. And it will be mine and Desmond's, when we're married next month. We're just on our way to the Valley now, so Desmond can attend to some business and I can attend a fitting for my wedding dress. And I'm stopping at my jeweler to have them polish the Green Goiter."

Cecily removed a scarf from her neck to reveal a gigantic emerald.

"Whoa," said Jaundice.

"I'd been keeping it in my train case, but Desmond advised me to put it on when this whole investigation started, so it's never out of my sight," Cecily explained. "Daddy bought the Goiter for Mummy when they were engaged, and now it's mine. I'm going to wear it when Desmond and I are married, so of course it needs to be *sparkling*."

"Have you ever had occasion to meet Mademoiselle Magique before today?" the great detective asked.

"I've never met her," said Cecily. She leaned toward the Bland Sisters conspiratorially. "Can she *really* read minds?"

"We can't reveal her secrets," said Jaundice.

"We took the Magician's Oath," Kale explained.

"Well, it's not as if there's much going on in my mind for anyone to read, anyway!" Cecily said, giggling.

The sisters nodded. They understood all too well.

Hugo Fromage smiled politely. "Can you tell me where you and your fiancé were, prior to the announcement of Mademoiselle Magique's disappearance?" he asked.

"I'd had a headache in the midst of lunch, so I was convalescing with Desmond in our compartment. Well, except for a few minutes, when I went out to powder my nose. It was just as I was returning that I heard the commotion in the dining car."

"*She* could have done something to Magique," Kale whispered to Jaundice. She put a question mark next to Miss Springwell's name in her notebook.

"So could her fiancé, since both of them were on their

own for a few minutes," Jaundice said. "Or maybe they were in it together! But why?"

"Could this be yours, then?" the great detective asked, holding out the handkerchief to Miss Springwell. She narrowed her green eyes to inspect it.

"Well, there's no *H* in Cecily Springwell, of course," she noted. She scratched her head again. "It is lovely, though."

"She scratches her head a lot," Kale whispered to her sister. "Maybe she has *lice*."

"Or maybe she's allergic to her hair spray," Jaundice whispered back. "She must use a lot. She never seems to have a hair out of place."

"It is lovely . . . to have made your acquaintance," Hugo Fromage said. "I appreciate your help."

"I don't see how a silly little thing like me could help you," said Cecily, laughing brightly.

"You are much more than a 'silly little thing,' *mademoiselle*," Hugo Fromage said. When Miss Springwell stood, the great detective also rose, took her hand, and looked into her emerald-green eyes. "Do not, as they say, sell yourself short."

☛ Professor Magic's Rules of Illusion ☚

The best magicians adapt to their environments.

▥▥▥▥▥▥▥▥▥▥▥▥ Chapter Thirteen ▥▥▥▥▥▥▥▥▥▥▥▥

I thought I'd heard of all the sleuths out there. I can't seem to recall a Hugo Fromage," said Desmond Goode. He had a newspaper under his arm as he took a seat across from the great detective.

"That is a pity," said Hugo Fromage. "For you."

"Well, we have quite a situation here, eh? The *Mentioner* is going to have a field day," Mr. Goode said, unfolding his paper and laying it on the table. "They always come up with such great headlines for their crime stories—today's was COPS TEASED; WEASEL FLEES. For this mystery, I'm imagining THE LADY VANISHES!"

"Ah, you are a clever one, Monsieur Goode," said the great detective. "Can you tell me where you were when the lady vanished?"

"I was in the compartment with Cecily after we returned from lunch and until the bell rang for tea, except for the time she excused herself to powder her nose," Mr. Goode explained. "You know how long it takes a woman to make herself presentable? Well, multiply that by ten for my Cecily! Sometimes I wonder how we manage to go anywhere or do anything, with the amount of time she spends off in the loo. 'It's a good thing you're easy on the eyes,' I tell her."

The young man chuckled at this. Hugo Fromage did not. Instead, he said, "Have you ever been on this train before, *monsieur?*"

"Well, yes. I travel frequently in my line of business," the young man explained.

"And what line of business is that?"

Desmond Goode produced a business card and handed it to the great detective. The Bland Sisters could see that it said:

"We import and export all manner of items: pottery, art, furniture. Whatever our clients request. I transport it by train to the docks at Uncanny Valley and see that it's packed onto a ship."

"And the reverse, I assume, if you are expecting imports from abroad?" asked the great detective.

"Sure, that's the ticket," said Mr. Goode. "My fiancée was right. You are sharp as a tack!"

Hugo Fromage bowed his head. "One more question, *s'il vous plaît*. Have you ever met Mademoiselle Magique, or anyone else on this train, prior to this journey?"

"Well, I met my fiancée on this train, of course. In this

very dining car, about six months ago. Once I caught a glimpse of those shining eyes, and heard that sparkling laugh, she'd stolen my heart."

"Anyone else?" asked the great detective.

"No one . . . except the conductor. I always see him on my travels between Dullsville and the Uncanny Valley," the young man said. He snapped his fingers several times. "Oh, what is his name?"

"Mr. Harold," said Kale, looking through her notes. "Frank Harold."

"Right, good old Mr. Harold," said Mr. Goode.

"You have been very helpful," said the great detective. He pulled out the monogrammed handkerchief. "By the way, do you know to whom this belongs?"

The young man took the handkerchief from Hugo Fromage and inspected it. "No, I don't," he said. "But I imagine it belongs to someone of some means. The embroidery is very fine."

"*Merci*," said the great detective. He took the handkerchief from Mr. Goode and placed it on the table between them. "I appreciate your time and consideration."

"At first, I thought he and Miss Springwell could have been up to something together. But he just seems like a normal businessman," said Jaundice, after Mr. Goode had left the dining car. Although Jaundice had never before met a businessman, normal or otherwise, she was sure she was right. She almost always was.

"A businessman with exceptional dental hygiene," said Kale, as she added this to her notes.

"If Mr. Goode's teeth are real," Hugo Fromage said, "they may be the only genuine thing about him."

☛ Professor Magic's Rules of Illusion ☚
If something goes wrong onstage,
always have a backup plan.

⊞⊞⊞⊞⊞⊞⊞⊞⊞⊞⊞ Chapter Fourteen ⊞⊞⊞⊞⊞⊞⊞⊞⊞⊞⊞

This is an *outrage!*" said Mr. Hatchett, storming into the dining car. "I have been sitting in my compartment all afternoon with no word as to whether or not they've cleared the tracks. What kind of outfit is this?"

"We do not work for the railroad, *monsieur*," explained the great detective. "But I can assure you, *our* work will not take long." He gestured to the seat across from him.

Reluctantly, Mr. Hatchett sat. "Well, I guess it doesn't matter. Other than the interview I did with Colonel McRobb, this whole trip has been a waste. Magique invited me to review her comeback performance at the Uncanny Valley

Hippodrome, and it looks like *that's* not going to happen. I've always said female magicians aren't up to the task. It seems this one made herself disappear before she produced another failure."

"Another failure?" asked Hugo Fromage.

"I panned her debut at the Dullsville Music Hall last year," he explained. "Total disaster. Several audience members walked out, and then the rest of the crowd turned on her. I've never heard such loud booing—or seen actual tomatoes being thrown."

"What made everyone get up and leave, and boo, and lob the tomatoes?" asked the great detective.

Mr. Hatchett pulled out his reporter's notebook and leafed through it. "It was in the middle of a goofy routine she called 'The Mind's Eye.' She claimed she could read the audience's thoughts. After she started with her silly 'readings,' some people had had it, I suppose. One man even shouted at her as he stormed out."

"What did he shout, if I might ask?" inquired the great detective.

Mr. Hatchett flipped his pen around his fingers as he scanned through his notes. "It was too dark in the music hall for me to see his face, or anyone else's, but everyone heard him. Ah, here it is. It was 'Balderdash.' As he left, the man shouted 'Balderdash.'"

Kale looked at Jaundice. Hadn't they heard the word "balderdash" somewhere before? She flipped through her notes.

"That was what Colonel McRobb said earlier," she whispered. "Balderdash!"

"Do you think that means *he* did it?" Jaundice wondered.

"Thank you," Hugo Fromage said to the reporter. "That will be all."

After Mr. Hatchett left the dining car, the great detective turned to the Bland Sisters.

"That will be all for you, too, *mademoiselles*," he said. He took a newspaper from the courtesy cart and began leafing through it.

"But, don't we need to continue our investigation?" Jaundice asked.

The great detective smiled. "You two have been very helpful. But I think we have gathered all of the necessary information."

"Would you like my notes?" Kale asked, offering her notebook. "Jaundice and I have found a few really good leads."

"I have made my own notes. Up here," the great detective said, pointing a gloved finger to his exceedingly round head. "Now that all of the ingredients are in place, it is time for Hugo Fromage to allow his brain stew to simmer."

"Well, if you need us for anything else, we'll be in our compartment," Jaundice reminded him, though he seemed too preoccupied with his newspaper to hear her.

"I'm not really a fan of stew, anyway," admitted Kale. She had tried it once, unsuccessfully, when the Bland Sisters were kidnapped by pirates. "Let alone brain stew."

☞ Professor Magic's Rules of Illusion ☜

Practice makes perfect.
Not just for magic, but for everything.

⊞⊞⊞⊞⊞⊞⊞⊞⊞⊞⊞⊞ Chapter Fifteen ⊞⊞⊞⊞⊞⊞⊞⊞⊞⊞⊞⊞⊞

The Bland Sisters leaned out the door between the dining car and the passenger car. A tow truck had just finished pulling the Fluff-O truck away, and several workmen from the train company were clearing away the broken barrels and using blowtorches to melt the last bits of marshmallow crème off the tracks and the train's wheels.

"Looks like they're almost finished," said Jaundice.

"Ah, well," said Kale, gazing longingly at the scene. She would have loved to help with the cleanup.

Back in the Bland Sisters' compartment, Jaundice made sure to tie the door shut with one of her trusty pieces of string, to make sure *they* wouldn't fall prey to any foul play. As she would one day learn when her first issue of *Nuts for Knots* finally arrived, she had just executed a more than decent "slipped constrictor."

"It's nice to be alone together, with no one needing our assistance," Jaundice noted.

"It is," said Kale. "Though I wish we had some socks to work on. The darning basket must be overflowing at home."

"Well, we've already tried admiring the scenery," said Jaundice. "And we've read the better part of *Professor Magic's Rules of Illusion*."

"I do wish I had *Tillie's Tips* to keep us company," Kale said.

"There has to be something we can do to pass the time," said Jaundice.

"There is the matter of Monsieur Fromage's investigation," Kale reminded her sister. She flipped through her notebook. "Though there is *a lot* to consider, starting with all the evidence: the red envelope, the burned paper, the bloody fabric, the green handkerchief embroidered with the letter *H* . . ."

"And the box of Good & Plenty. Don't forget that," Jaundice said. Kale added it to the list. "And then there's all the suspects."

"There are *so many* of them. And most of them were

unattended when she disappeared," Kale said, showing Jaundice her notes. "Miss Springwell and Mr. Goode, the countess, Mr. Harold, even Vera Dreary was alone for a few moments when she went to fetch the cream. The only two who say they were together were Colonel McRobb and Kirk Hatchett."

"They *say* they were together," said Jaundice. "But *were* they?"

"We know Colonel McRobb was the one who said 'balderdash.' Doesn't that mean he was the one who stormed out of Magique's show?" Kale asked.

The Bland Sisters blinked at each other.

"Whoa," said Kale, holding her head. She couldn't remember the last time she'd used that much brainpower.

"Is it just me, or are we starting to sound like real detectives?" Jaundice asked.

"Well, if we are, we have our work cut out for us," Kale said. "We also have to figure out who stole Countess Goudenoff's ring. Everyone on this train seems suspicious."

"Except for us and Monsieur Fromage," said Jaundice.

Kale closed her notebook and put her head down on the table. Even if this kind of accounting didn't involve numbers, it still left her with a headache.

Jaundice put her head down on the table, too. The Bland Sisters sat in silence for several minutes. Finally, Kale spoke.

"Three," she said.

"Six," said Jaundice.

"Nine."

"Twelve."

On they went with their numbers divisible by three—until eventually (and not surprisingly), they both fell asleep yet again.

This time, Kale was still doing her best to rescue whoever was buried beneath the dust and clutter. After a great deal of effort, two hands finally appeared. Kale grabbed them and pulled as hard as she could. Eventually, the endangered party emerged . . .

. . . and it turned out to be none other than the Bland Sisters' parents.

"Finally," said their mother, dusting herself off.

"It's about time," said their father. "You and your sister packed us away long enough."

"Packed you away?" Kale said. She turned to Jaundice. "Does that make *any* sense to you?"

But Jaundice didn't look like herself; she looked like a long piece of string, with a knot where her head should be.

"I'm a frayed knot," she said.

At the same time, Jaundice was dreaming that the phone, as ever, was still ringing urgently, and seemingly close by.

Ring-ring! Ring-ring!

This time, the Bland Sisters' parents were standing over Jaundice.

"I don't know why you keep expecting them to pick it up," said their father.

"I'm right here!" Jaundice shouted, waving her arms. But their parents didn't seem to notice.

Their mother sighed. "Oh, well. I guess there's always Plan B," she said.

"Right," said their father. "I'd forgotten about Plan B."

Suddenly, Jaundice found herself in the red wagon with Kale, being pulled by their parents at a breakneck speed, on a steep incline. Up, up, up they went, their parents running faster and faster.

"Here goes nothing," said their father.

They were just about at the top, where the incline dropped off into a valley of what seemed like nothingness.

"I don't like this at all!" Kale said, whimpering.

"Please, stop!" Jaundice cried.

"Well, if you insist," said their mother.

"Hold on tight!" cried their father. "Things are about to get interesting!"

And then they disappeared.

Jaundice and Kale were still in the wagon, and the wagon was airborne.

The Bland Sisters woke up with a jolt.

It took a moment for Jaundice to realize she wasn't still in midair.

"Did you feel that?" she asked.

"I did," said Kale, exhaling. She was glad her sister was there for her, in dreams and in real life, and that Jaundice now looked a lot less stringy.

The Bland Sisters put their hands over their hearts.

"I dreamed about our parents," Jaundice said. "And now I've got that ache again."

"Me, too," said Kale. "In my dream, they told me we'd 'packed them away.' Whatever that means."

"In my dream, they kept trying to call someone," Jaundice explained. "I think that someone was us. Then I dreamed you and I were flying. It was scary at first, and then, it felt . . ."

"What?" Kale asked.

Jaundice thought for a moment.

"It's times like these I wish we had our dictionary with us," said Jaundice. "I think the word I'm looking for is . . . exhilarating?"

"Whoa," said Kale. *Exhilarating* was a word she wasn't sure she could spell, let alone experience.

"But then I woke up. I wish I knew what happened next," said Jaundice.

A whistle pierced the air.

"Did you hear that?" Kale asked.

"I did," said Jaundice. "What do you think it means?"

Kale opened the curtain and looked out at the landscape. "Well, either the trees are moving, or we are."

Mr. Harold appeared in their doorway. "The tracks are finally clear, so we're on our way," he said. "We should be in the Uncanny Valley in about an hour. In the meantime, Mr. Fromage would like to see everyone in the dining car. Including both of you."

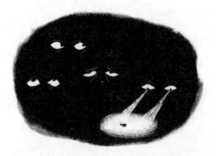

Magic is about noticing little details
that others don't take the time to see or understand.

Chapter Sixteen

The great detective was seated with his back to the Bland Sisters when they first entered the dining car. As they walked around him to take their seats, they could see his mustache and shoes looked particularly shiny, and he was wearing a fresh flower in his little vase-shaped lapel pin.

The Bland Sisters considered the suspects. Cecily and Desmond were already seated, and Cecily was whispering in Desmond's ear. An anxious Vera Dreary helped the countess to her chair. Kirk Hatchett and Colonel McRobb appeared last, and they each seemed more disgruntled than ever.

"Everyone looks guilty," Jaundice whispered.

"Well, they can't *all* have done it," said Kale. "How silly would *that* be?"

"This better not take long, Fromage," the colonel said. "I have a bookstore full of *True Hero* fans waiting for me. I'm sure the line for my signing is out the door by now."

Desmond Goode rolled his eyes. "We *all* have business to attend to," he said. Cecily squeezed his hand.

"We have our socks waiting for us, for instance," Jaundice said.

"A *lot* of socks, I'm sure," Kale added. "And we only have one darning egg between us."

Hugo Fromage stood up and cleared his throat. "*Mesdames et messieurs*, I thank you for indulging me this afternoon and evening. It has been quite illuminating, speaking to you all. In fact, I think I can reveal, without a doubt, what has happened to our errant magician. Let us start, first, with the evidence."

The great detective gestured to the table beside him, on which the embroidered handkerchief, the torn bit of robe, the box of Good & Plenty, the red envelope, and the scrap of burned paper were laid. He held up the bit of robe with his gloved fingers.

"A magician's robe, smeared with what is no doubt blood, her train compartment ransacked. She is nowhere to be found on the Uncanny Express, and there is no way she could have willingly leaped off the train, given its speed. So how can we account for this? The rest of the clues tell a story."

The Bland Sisters sighed. They loved a good story.

"The burned scrap of paper, it turns out, is a clipping from the *Mentioner*—specifically, the advertisement for Mademoiselle Magique's comeback performance," Hugo Fromage informed the group. He opened his copy of today's newspaper to reveal the matching ad. "There is writing across this clipping. One can make out the words 'STOP, OR EL' from the letters that remain legible: 'STOP, OR ELSE,' I suspect. Someone did not want her to appear at the Hippodrome this afternoon. But who? Then, Hugo Fromage allows his brain stew to simmer. He remembers the magician's outburst at lunch, and her mention of secrets waiting to be revealed. He remembers what was recounted by Monsieur Hatchett, the reporter who was in attendance six months ago at Mademoiselle Magique's fateful show in Dullsville. People walked out, Monsieur Hatchett said. Just as the magician was starting to perform her mind-reading trick. I believe something was said that night that had a ring of truth to it."

"You mean, Magique really can read minds?" Kale asked.

"The act of mind reading is a great deal like detective work," explained Hugo Fromage. "One must only be observant, and clues will appear. Just by looking out at her audience, I am sure the magician could have made some

observations, and from those observations came connections, and from those connections came conjecture. For instance, what were the psychic claims she made to her audience during her performance last year?"

"I think she told us, but I didn't start taking notes until after she disappeared," Kale said. "There was something about two people in love and something else about a woman committing a crime."

"And a man who is hiding something," Jaundice added.

Mr. Hatchett twirled his pen. "I have it in *my* notes from that night," he said, consulting his reporter's notebook. "She looked out into the audience and said, 'two young people in love are deceiving each other,' then 'a woman has committed a grave crime against her husband,' then 'a man with a limp is hiding something.' Pretty vague stuff. That's how these fakers work."

"I wonder, though, if there was some grain of truth to those claims," the great detective suggested. "Perhaps Mademoiselle Magique did not know it, but what she meant as a vague reading actually touched a nerve with members of her audience. Perhaps that is why they left her performance—not because of her shoddy showmanship, but to escape the revealing of their transgressions!"

Everyone in the dining car shifted in his or her seat. Colonel McRobb scoffed and crossed his arms. Chrysanthemum yawned.

"In honor of Mademoiselle Magique, Hugo Fromage will perform his *own* magic. With you all as my audience, I will solve the mystery of the magician's disappearance using nothing but the physical evidence before me, the testimony I have gathered during my questioning of you all this afternoon, the help of my faithful assistants, and, of course, the slow and steady simmering of my brain stew," the great detective announced. "Let us take the matter of the handkerchief, which no one will claim. To whom does it belong?"

Hugo Fromage picked up the handkerchief and unfurled it. As he held it up for all to see, he looked a lot like a magician himself, Kale thought.

"It is too ornate for the countess, and too fancy for Mademoiselle Dreary, and Mademoiselle Springwell does not claim it. And it is embroidered with an *H*, which no woman has in their initials. So curious. And then, I wonder, what if someone on this train is not using their real name?"

The great detective's gaze fell on Cecily Springwell.

"*Mademoiselle*, do you have something you would like to tell us?" he asked.

"I don't know what you mean," said Cecily, scratching her head. "All of this is really rather boring," she said with a giggle.

"I do not think you find it boring at all, *mademoiselle*. Nor do I think you are as foolish as you pretend to be," said the great detective. "Nor do I think it is a coincidence that the embroidery on this handkerchief matches perfectly with your green eyes."

"Darling, what's he on about?" Desmond asked Cecily.

"Simply that your fiancée is not the heiress Cecily Springwell," said the detective. "She is Hortense Frank, one half of the detective team known as Harry and Hortense!"

"Well, I guess the jig is up," said Hortense, sighing. She pulled off her blond wig, revealing her short dark hair. "At least I don't have to wear this anymore. It itches something awful."

"I guess she doesn't have lice, then," Kale said, crossing it off in her notebook.

"So, who is the other half of the detective team?" asked Jaundice.

"That . . . would be me," said Mr. Harold.

"So you're not really 'Frank Harold'?" asked Kale.

"Close. I'm Harry Frank," he explained. "We've been undercover for just over six months now, trying to crack our latest case—a thief who's been stealing jewelry and artwork and other valuables all over Dullsville. The paper's been calling him 'the Weasel.' How did you know it was us?"

"What kind of a detective would I be, were I not familiar with my contemporaries?" Hugo Fromage explained. "Plus, there was the woman's voice saying, 'She's going to ruin everything,' which Mademoiselle Dreary said she heard in the hallway, only to find you standing there with the tea tray, Monsieur Frank. This coincides with the time Madame Frank left her compartment to 'powder her nose.' I suspect you two were whispering out there, and that Madame Frank ducked into the restroom when Mademoiselle Dreary appeared on the scene."

"When I saw Harry walk by with the tea tray, I did excuse myself," Hortense Frank admitted. "It seemed like the perfect opportunity to confront Magique together and beg her not to reveal our identities, for the good of our investigation."

"But when we knocked on her compartment door, she wasn't there," Harry Frank continued. "I must admit, the possibility of more than six months of undercover work going to waste made me a little, er, emotional. Hortense had given me her handkerchief to dry my eyes when the maid appeared. I must have dropped it in my panic."

"All that effort I put into my disguise, and I forgot to buy new handkerchiefs," Hortense Frank said, shaking her head.

"Does that mean that Mr. Goode is . . . the Weasel?" Jaundice asked.

"An astute observation, *mademoiselle*," said the great detective.

"That is *preposterous!*" Desmond Goode exclaimed.

"Is it?" asked Hugo Fromage. "You operate a mysterious import-export business, making it easy to relocate the stolen treasures. You are obsessed with reading about crime in the newspapers. And of course, your last name: Goode. As the newspapers have described, the man the authorities are looking for is named Clayton Plenty."

"Goode . . . and Plenty," Jaundice said, reaching for the candy box.

"Do you think Magique was trying to give us a clue?" Kale wondered.

"I suspect she was. I suspect you are also familiar with this candy, Monsieur Plenty. And that it is what inspired your latest alias," added the great detective.

"Too clever by half," Clayton Plenty said. "Don't believe a word he says, Cecily—er, whatever your real name is."

"Oh, please. You never loved Cecily," said Hortense. "For all your talk about her shining eyes and her sparkling laugh, the real object of your desire was the Green Goiter. Harry and

I knew you'd been smuggling your stolen loot on the train and handing it off to your contact in the Uncanny Valley, who ships it off to prospective buyers. And we knew you liked cozying up to rich girls and making off with their valuables."

"So, you just made up 'Cecily Springwell,' and 'Fernwood'?" asked Kale, consulting her notes.

"Not exactly," said Hortense. "The real Cecily was my roommate in college; she's away on vacation, so she said she didn't mind if I impersonated her here for a little while. All Harry had to do was get a job on the Uncanny Express, to keep an eye on you, Mr. Plenty. And all I had to do was lure you in . . . which didn't take long."

"How could it?" he said, gazing forlornly at Hortense.

"I waited until you came up with a reason for me to take the Green Goiter out of the safe at home," Hortense continued. "When you offered to take me to the Uncanny Valley to have it cleaned, I knew you were ready to make your move. And you would have, too, if our cover wasn't just blown!"

"Who says he hasn't made his move?" said the great detective. He turned to Jaundice. "*Mademoiselle*, if you would be so kind as to look in Monsieur Plenty's briefcase."

When Jaundice opened the briefcase, something glittering and green caught her eye.

"The Goiter!" exclaimed Hortense. Her hand flew to the jewel around her neck. "But, then, what am I wearing now?"

"That one is fake, I am afraid," said Hugo Fromage. "Though I suspect the one Monsieur Plenty stole from you while you went to 'powder your nose' earlier is also a fake, no?"

Hortense blushed. "Cecily has the real one with her," she explained.

"I can't believe I'm finally going to jail for stealing a *fake* emerald," said Clayton.

"During her reading, Magique said, 'two young people in love are deceiving each other,'" Kale said. "And she was right!"

"Desmond—or, rather, *Clayton*—took me to her show on our first date," Hortense explained. "When the magician gave that reading, I was worried it would make him suspicious, so I faked one of my headaches so he would take me home."

"Wait. There's something else in his suitcase, too," said Jaundice. She pulled out a ring set with a dark red stone.

"My garnet ring!" exclaimed the countess.

Clayton Plenty shrugged. "I couldn't resist," he admitted.

"I told you I di'n't do nuffin'," Vera reminded her.

"No, you did not take anything from Countess Goudenoff. But your employer did take something precious from you, Mademoiselle Dreary," said the great detective. "Might you show everyone the framed photo Count Goudenoff gave you, before his passing?"

"It's right here," said Vera, producing it from a pocket in her tweedy coat. She handed it to Hugo Fromage.

"The last thing the count said to you before he died was, 'I'll always look after you,' yes?" said the great detective, gazing at the photo. He then popped it out of its frame.

"Oh, don't break it!" said Vera. "It's the only one I have!"

"Just as I thought," said Hugo Fromage. From behind the photo, he produced a folded-up piece of paper. He unfolded it and adjusted his pince-nez to read it. "It is the Last Will and Testament of Count Goudenoff, in which he leaves everything to you . . . his daughter!"

At this, Vera Dreary fainted.

⟜ Professor Magic's Rules of Illusion ⟜

To add one final amazing moment to your performance,
nothing beats a costume change.

Chapter Seventeen

S omeone fetch some smelling salts!" shouted the great detective. Harry Frank soon appeared with a vial, which he placed under Vera Dreary's nose.

"Who? How? What?" she said, sitting up straight.

"How did you know?" Kale asked Hugo Fromage.

"I told you, being a detective involves using your eyes and ears," the great detective reminded her. "In this case, it was Mademoiselle Dreary's ears that gave her away. They are quite distinct," noted the great detective.

"They are funny little things," Vera said, patting her ears self-consciously.

"Well, those 'funny little things' are identical to the count's," said Hugo Fromage. "When I saw his photo, I began to have my suspicions. But when the dog Chrysanthemum vomited on my shoes, it was then that Hugo Fromage knew for sure."

"Come again?" said Vera Dreary.

"The vomit, it smelled terrible," said the great detective. "But it also smelled faintly of something else: bitter almonds. I suspect that the dog had lapped up some of the tea that was spilled this afternoon, around the time of Mademoiselle Magique's disappearance. That tea was poisoned with cyanide."

Everyone turned to look at Vera Dreary.

"Why's everyone lookin' at me?" she asked. "I di'n't do nuffin'!"

"No, you didn't, mademoiselle," said Hugo Fromage. "She did."

He pointed his finger at Countess Goudenoff.

"You deliberately ordered milk for the tea and then demanded that Mademoiselle Dreary fetch the cream. While she was gone, you poured the poison into her tea. When you learned there would be an investigation into Mademoiselle Magique's disappearance, you feared an exposure of your own attempted crime, so you deliberately spilled the tea onto the floor," said the great detective.

"He told me Vera was his daughter, and that he'd written her into a new will—after I did him in, I searched everywhere for it. I couldn't risk that it would be found and she would be named his heir. I'd never part with that money!" the countess said.

"You killed the count?" Jaundice asked.

"Indeed, she did," said the great detective. He took the countess's ring from Jaundice and fiddled with the garnet. Eventually, it popped open. "And I suspect she hid the poison in here."

"'A woman has committed a grave crime against her husband,'" Jaundice recalled. "That's the second reading Magique gave."

"My husband had bought us tickets to her show for our last anniversary," the countess admitted. "Ironically, I thought it would be foolish to let them go to waste after his death; I had Vera accompany me, so I could keep an eye on her. When that 'magician' started in on her reading, I worried that Vera might suspect me, so I told her I found the performance tiring and needed to leave immediately—which wasn't untrue."

"And I think you were the one who left the threatening note for Mademoiselle Magique," said the great detective, holding up the red envelope. "With your crimson lipstick and nails and your garnet ring, red seems to be your favorite color."

"You are not as dumb as you look, Monsieur Fromage. Clearly, I underestimated you," said the countess.

"Most people do," the great detective said with a nod.

"You—you *monster*," said Vera. "Me mum always said the count was too good for you!"

"He wasn't too good for your mum, evidently," growled the countess.

"Me mum also said, 'That Ima was never good enough to be a Goudenoff!'" Vera Dreary cried. "Now I hope they take away your title, so you'll have to go back to your maiden name: Nutt!"

"*Ima Nutt?*" Jaundice said.

"Don't be so hard on yourself," said Kale, patting Jaundice's hand.

"What about Magique?" Jaundice asked the countess. "Did you kill her, too, to keep her from revealing your secrets?"

"I am getting to that," said Hugo Fromage. "But first, I must ask Colonel McRobb two questions. The first is: How is your leg feeling?"

"It hurts like heck, like any war wound," the colonel replied.

"The second question is: Which leg?"

"Pardon me?" said the colonel.

"Which leg did you break on your heroic and daring

rescue mission?" asked the great detective. "Because I have seen you limp on one, and then the other, throughout our time on this train. This makes me think that the answer may be neither."

"Well, I *never*," the colonel said, rising from his chair.

"Exactly. You have a great deal riding on your reputation as a 'true hero,'" Hugo Fromage noted. "It would be an even greater tragedy if your story turned out to be *un*true."

"I don't need to listen to this balderdash!" the colonel said, his face redder than ever.

"Balderdash!" Kale repeated, showing everyone where she'd underlined the word in her notes. "That was what one of the audience members said as he stormed out of Magique's show!"

"So what if I was there? My editor gave me a ticket, to celebrate *True Hero*'s first week on the bestseller list. Attending a performance is not a crime. Now, I'm going back to my compartment!" said the colonel, striding off.

"Before you do, sir, you have forgotten something," the great detective said. "Two things, in fact."

Jaundice followed Hugo Fromage's gaze.

"His walking stick!" she said.

"Yes," said the great detective. "In his haste to escape the truth, he has left behind his walking stick. And his limp altogether."

"'A man with a limp is hiding something,'" recalled Kale. "That was Magique's third reading!"

Everyone in the room stared at the colonel. Finally, he sank into the nearest chair.

"All right then, here it is: I never saw active duty during the war," he explained. "I worked at a desk job, filing paperwork and daydreaming about the heroic adventures I might have had. And then, long after the war was over, I fell

off a ladder while pruning some hedges and broke my ankle pretty badly. After it healed and I was up and around and using my walking stick, I got a lot of sympathy from people—and respect, even from perfect strangers, who assumed I was injured in combat. So I started writing down the adventures I'd imagined all those years ago, and they seemed so vivid, they became real to me. 'Colonel McRobb' was born. Until now, no one ever asked me if it was all true or not. People will believe anything, if you tell them with enough authority."

"So *you* did something to Magique," Kale said. "To protect your secrets."

"Despite what my memoir claims, I've never hurt anyone in my life. I followed her on this train to *bribe* her, not kill her," the colonel said. He opened his briefcase to reveal rows of stacked bills. "The insufferable woman went and disappeared before I could make my offer!"

"Well, then," said Hugo Fromage. "All of you were in the audience at Mademoiselle Magique's debut performance six months ago. All of you witnessed her mind-reading act and felt singled out by that reading. All of you got up and left, which caused the rest of the crowd to reach for their tomatoes. The magician has kept a low profile since then, recovering from her failure and planning her comeback—until recently, when she advertised her return to the stage, and to the mind-reading act that implicated you all. I would not even be surprised if she sent you all tickets to her comeback performance, to goad you into attending."

"Now I'm really confused," Kale said, rifling through her notes. "Does this really mean they all did it?"

"It is quite possible, *mademoiselle*," said the great detective. The other passengers began protesting as he turned to them. "You all knew she would be on this train, you all made sure you were passengers today, and you all had reason to stop her, by whatever means necessary. Including you, Monsieur Hatchett. *Especially* you."

"Me?" Mr. Hatchett scoffed. "That hack managed to kill her career all by herself. She didn't need any help from me."

"Ah, but you relished writing your terrible review of the occasion. It is clear that you feel quite a disdain for Mademoiselle Magique. What is not immediately clear is the reason, although I have my suspicions," said the great detective.

Mr. Hatchett laughed nervously and twirled his pen around his fingers. "I bet you do," he said.

"You, who are always in the habit of exhibiting such flamboyance with your pen, not to mention such dexterity. You yourself have a few tricks up your sleeve, do you not?" said Hugo Fromage. "Could you have been an aspiring magician yourself at one point? Might you even have been a potential protégé of Mademoiselle Magique's father, Professor Magic, who ultimately dismissed you for having inferior skills?"

Mr. Hatchett turned red. "I—I don't know what you're talking about," he said.

"I think you do. I think you have sought revenge against Professor Magic for many years and have finally found an outlet for your anger in the ruining of his daughter's career. Perhaps that frustration went just a bit too far this afternoon?"

Mr. Hatchett looked around at everyone else, who were all looking at him.

"Please, I—I didn't do anything, other than write that bad review last year," Mr. Hatchett said. "You can't blame me, after how the old man treated me. He said I'd never be a magician, that my fingers weren't quick enough. He destroyed my confidence. And then his daughter thinks she can make a name for herself? A *female* magician, of all things? Anyone can tell you that women don't have the flair necessary for the magical arts. They do not possess the authority to arrest the audience."

"Those are intriguing theories," said the great detective. "Perhaps you will enjoy developing them further from the inside of a jail cell, once you tell me what you have done with Mademoiselle Magique!"

At this, Mr. Hatchett started crying.

"Wait," said Kale, reviewing her notes. Then she looked at the passenger manifest and the compartment diagram. "I'm having a Feeling."

Jaundice peered over her shoulder. "What?" she asked.

"Hugo Fromage said that everyone in this room is a passenger on this train. But there are ten people in the room now and ten names listed as passengers, *including* Magique," Kale said. Fortunately, doing the math didn't give Kale a headache, as it so often did. "That means one person here isn't on the manifest or the compartment diagram."

"Who?" asked Vera Dreary.

Kale looked up. "Hugo Fromage."

"Hold on," Harry Frank said, taking the clipboard from Kale and looking it over. "She's right. Your name isn't here, sir."

"That's because I boarded the train when it stopped," explained the great detective.

"But it's an *express* train. It has no stops," said Jaundice. "Unless you boarded the train after it ran into the Fluff-O."

"He was already here when the accident happened," Kale remembered. "He was offering to help us find Magique when we felt the crash."

Everyone turned to look at the great detective. He smiled. He removed his pince-nez. He removed his homburg hat.

Then he removed his mustache.

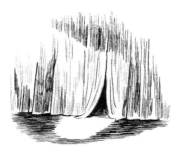

☛ Professor Magic's Rules of Illusion ☚
Magic effects demonstrate the impossible.
Escapes, on the other hand, are real.

⊞⊞⊞⊞⊞⊞⊞⊞⊞ Chapter Eighteen ⊞⊞⊞⊞⊞⊞⊞⊞⊞

V oilà!"

For a good few seconds, no one in the dining car
spoke. It was Kale who finally broke the shocked silence.

"Magique . . . is that . . . you?" she asked.

"Of course," said the magician. She pulled off the bald
cap, revealing her silver hair, and stepped out of a well-padded
suit. "I told you I had a plan."

"But, why?" asked Jaundice.

"At my last performance, I was humiliated when the
audience turned on me, after some people began to walk
out during my mind-reading act. I vowed to find out why.

So I spent the past six months tracking everyone down and looking into their lives, their stories, and most important, their secrets. And, of course, I wanted to thumb my nose at *certain reviewers* who said 'women don't have the flair necessary for the magical arts,' and that we don't have 'the authority to arrest the audience.' Well, I certainly convinced you that I had the 'authority' to 'arrest' you a few moments ago, Mr. Hatchett. And I did it with more than a little 'flair.'"

"You violated the Magician's Oath," Kale reminded the reporter. She tried to remember the exact words. "It says, 'I will extend nothing but respect and goodwill to my fellow magicians . . .'"

"'For as long as I might wave my wand,'" Jaundice added.

"You two *have* been paying attention," Magique said proudly.

Mr. Hatchett set his pen on the table in front of him. He hung his head.

"It was an astonishing performance," said Hortense Frank. "How did you manage to pull it off?"

"After Jaundice and Kale left my compartment, I made sure it would look suspicious, so I burned the threatening note from Countess Goudenoff, tossed my belongings everywhere, and tore a bit of my robe and smeared it with raspberry jam from the dining car," Magique explained. "Then I ducked into the luggage car and hid inside my disappearing cabinet while I transformed myself. All I had to do was turn my satchel inside out to look like just another piece of luggage, and . . ."

"Voilà," repeated Jaundice. "So, is there really a great detective named Hugo Fromage?"

The magician laughed. "No," she admitted. "He is a work of fiction. As a certain military man once said, 'People will believe anything, if you tell them with enough authority.'"

She turned to the other passengers. "For the innocent among you, I am sorry for the inconvenience. But it was all in the name of justice—both criminal and poetic. I promised you all an 'astonishing performance' today. I hope I succeeded."

And then she turned to the Bland Sisters. "I told you that the mind is our most powerful tool. And that if we use it often and well, it will tell us many things and show us many secrets. Perhaps my greatest feat was getting you two to put your minds to work—in doing so, you solved the ultimate mystery!"

At this point, everyone in the room who wasn't on the verge of being arrested stood up and started clapping for Magique, and for Jaundice and Kale. Even Mr. McRobb rose to his feet and applauded, however begrudgingly. The magician began to cry as she took a well-deserved bow. Hortense Frank lent Magique her infamous handkerchief. The Bland Sisters tried to smile at the crowd as they covered their ears. They had never heard applause before; it sounded more than a bit like thunder.

"So if this was the 'astonishing performance' you promised, does that mean there won't be a show at the Hippodrome today?" asked Kale.

"Oh, you bet there will," said Magique. "Where else do you think I'd kick off my world tour?"

It was at this moment, amid all the excitement, that Clayton Plenty quietly slid under a table, crawled through the applauding crowd, and was about to sprint for the nearest exit. Unfortunately for him, it was at the very next moment that he was noticed.

"Stop! Thief!" cried Vera Dreary.

Mr. Plenty thought he still had a chance, so he made a break for it . . . until something tripped him up, and he landed flat on his back. That something was a handful of Good & Plenty candies, scattered across the floor by Jaundice.

"Oof," the thief groaned.

Jaundice reached into one of her smock pockets and pulled out a length of string.

"Now you're bound to stay put," she said, binding Clayton Plenty's hands in what she would later learn was a modified "handcuff knot." She really was a natural at this knot-tying thing.

"Just make sure the *Mentioner* gives my capture a good headline," the thief begged. "Might I suggest POP GOES THE WEASEL?"

☞ Professor Magic's Rules of Illusion ☜

Done well, magic provides its audience
with a dazzling, indelible memory.

Chapter Nineteen

When the train finally reached the station, the Uncanny Valley Police were waiting to arrest both the thief Clayton Plenty and Ima Nutt, the murderess formerly known as Countess Goudenoff.

"I can't believe I was foiled by a *magician*," Ima said, as she was led off in handcuffs.

"If things don't work out with your husband, you know where to find me," said Clayton, blowing kisses to Hortense.

"Talk about criminally insane," said Hortense. She turned to her husband. "Shall we go have a nice dinner, darling?"

"Yes, lovey," said Harry, kissing her cheek. "We have a brand-new case to discuss, after all."

"So, what do I call you, now that we know you're not a colonel?" Kirk Hatchett asked McRobb.

"My first name is Donald," McRobb confessed.

"Well, unfortunately, Donald, we're going to have to scrap your profile in the *Mentioner*," Mr. Hatchett told him. "I want to make up for my previous scathing review of Magique by writing all about her astounding comeback. And then, I'm afraid, I'll be writing an exposé of your fraud."

"Well, my career is finished, no thanks to that . . . woman," grumbled Mr. McRobb. He tossed his walking stick into a nearby trash can. "At least this means I can go back to taking ballroom dancing lessons. I was never much of a soldier, but I was deadly on the dance floor."

"Not so fast," said Kirk Hatchett. "Even if *True Hero* turned out to be completely false, you are a *cracking* good writer. Have you ever thought of trying your hand at fiction?"

Donald McRobb's face brightened. "A murder mystery, perhaps? With dancing? Ooh, I could call it *Tango of Terror!*" he suggested. The two men walked off, discussing the possibilities.

"I think I'll stay for the performance," said Vera Dreary, who was now wearing her former employer's pearls and mink

stole. "For the first time in a long time, I have nuffin' to do for anyone."

"Woof!" said Chrysanthemum. She seemed much happier in her new owner's arms.

"Enjoy," said Jaundice.

"Aren't you staying on?" said Magique. "I'll need help on my tour—especially a couple of assistants as observant and quick-thinking as you two."

The Bland Sisters couldn't help smiling. *Observant* and *quick-thinking* were not words they would use to describe themselves. Not before today, anyway.

"We should really get home," said Jaundice.

Kale nodded. "We have a sock-darning business to get back to, after all," she said.

"Well, at least stay for the performance. The train back to Dullsville doesn't leave for another few hours," said Magique. "In the meantime, let me introduce you girls to someone."

A young woman dressed all in black was wheeling the disappearing cabinet off the train at that very moment. The magician waved her over.

"Hey," Albertine said. She was a few years older than the Bland Sisters, and she looked a lot like Magique, except her hair was dark, and she seemed to like wearing a lot of eyeliner.

"Jaundice, Kale, this is my daughter," Magique said, giving Albertine a wink. "And my partner in crime."

"Wait," said Jaundice. "I thought you said you fired Albertine?"

"That was all part of the performance," the magician explained. "I needed you two on board to act as my assistants."

"And besides, I was, *ahem*, busy," Albertine said. She brought out a paper bag. "I figured you'd all be hungry before the show, so I brought dinner. Sorry it's just sandwiches."

"We love sandwiches, actually," said Jaundice.

"Well, bring them along. Albertine and I don't have much time to get ready," said Magique. "I've saved you two seats in the front row!"

The Hippodrome was the hugest building the Bland Sisters had ever seen.

"Look at all those bricks and windows," said Kale.

"Look at all those lights," said Jaundice, squinting.

Inside was no less astounding. Hundreds and hundreds of seats filled the room, each one upholstered in red velvet. The walls and the columns on either side of the stage were trimmed in gold. The ceiling featured a fresco of cherubs singing and frolicking and playing musical instruments.

"Those babies are certainly talented," noted Jaundice.

The Bland Sisters craned their necks to take it all in as they unwrapped their sandwiches. Tentatively, each of them took a bite.

"It tastes like . . . peanut butter," Kale decided. She had only ever had peanut butter before their parents left, and that was a long time ago.

"And something else," noted Jaundice. She lifted the top of the sandwich. "Something sweet. And white. And sticky."

The Bland Sisters looked at each other.

"*Marshmallow crème*," they said.

"Wait," said Kale. "Albertine made us these sandwiches. She said she had another job to do today. That's why she couldn't assist Magique on the train. Do you think . . ."

"I do," said Jaundice. "I do think. She's the one who parked that Fluff-O truck near the train tracks and overturned those barrels, to give Magique more time for her 'performance.'"

The Bland Sisters blinked at each other.

"Whoa," said Kale.

"I know," said Jaundice. "There we go, acting like detectives again."

"It's funny. The more we use our brains, the less painful it seems," said Kale.

Jaundice nodded. "This doesn't taste anything like a cheese sandwich," she noted.

"You're right," said Kale. "It's different in just about every way."

"I don't think I like it," said Jaundice.

"Me, neither," said Kale. "One bite is enough."

"Though that's one bite more than we would have taken before this trip," noted Jaundice.

"True," said Kale. "That's something."

The Bland Sisters rewrapped their fluffernutters and placed them underneath their seats. Suddenly, all around them, the lights started flickering.

"Uh-oh," said Kale.

The lights began to dim.

"What's happening?" said Jaundice.

The audience applauded, so Jaundice and Kale clapped, too. Then the orchestra started playing, and a spotlight fell on the back of the auditorium. Everyone in the audience turned around.

"Whoa," said Kale.

Albertine appeared in a tuxedo, wheeling out a large purple cannon painted with silver and gold stars. As she lit the cannon's fuse, the orchestra played a drumroll. Then . . .

BANG!

Magique shot from the cannon in a shower of glitter, soared over the audience, her purple and silver robes billowing, and landed gracefully onstage. The orchestra played a triumphant fanfare.

"Good evening, ladies and gentlemen!" she said. "Are you ready to witness the impossible?"

Amid the applause, she strode over to a black table, on which a single pack of cards was placed. As the orchestra played a waltz, the Queen of Magic shuffled, the cards cascading from one hand to the other. She cut the cards, then asked someone from the audience to pick one from the deck. Many people raised their hands, and Magique chose her volunteer: Vera Dreary.

"This *is* my lucky day!" she exclaimed. She climbed onstage with Chrysanthemum still in her arms. Vera chose the three of clubs and showed it to the audience, careful not to let the magician see. Magique shuffled the deck, cut the cards, and shuffled them again. Then she lifted a card off the top. She showed Vera and the audience.

"Is THIS your card?" Magique asked. It was the eight of diamonds.

"I'm sorry to say, it isn't," said Vera.

Magique seemed shaken.

"Oh no!" whispered Jaundice. Kale covered her eyes.

"Wait," said Magique. "What's this?"

She reached into Chrysanthemum's ear, and pulled something out.

"That's it!" cried Vera. "That's my card!"

"Woof!" exclaimed Chrysanthemum.

The audience erupted into applause again. The Bland Sisters breathed sighs of relief.

Magique performed one astonishing card trick after another. Then the lighting onstage changed, and the orchestra began playing a sinister tune. The magician brought Albertine onstage and levitated her, then sawed her in half. After Albertine emerged unscathed and the clapping died down, Magique addressed the audience.

"I owe those last two illusions to my father, Albertus Magnus, rest his soul," she explained. She bowed her head for a moment, then showed the audience a handbill from one of her father's performances. "He never thought I'd make a good magician. Or that any woman would."

Magique began folding up the handbill.

"But by discouraging me, he gave me an even greater gift—" she continued.

Smaller, and smaller, and smaller, she folded the handbill, until it seemed to disappear altogether.

"—the determination to prove him wrong."

She opened her hands. In a flash of color, dozens of butterflies flew out. The audience went wild.

"Thank you," said Magique, bowing. "Thank you. That illusion is all my own, as is this next one, where I will be assisted again by my daughter, Albertine, a talented magician in her own right."

Albertine appeared, wheeling the disappearing cabinet onstage.

"Now, I will need two volunteers from the audience," the magician announced.

Again, many people raised their hands. Magique looked around. Then she looked down at Jaundice and Kale.

"I think these two girls will do nicely," she said.

"But—we didn't even raise our hands," Jaundice said, as Magique and Albertine pulled them onstage.

Magique opened the cabinet and showed the audience its interior. She coughed dramatically.

"Oh, this cabinet is so dusty! If only I knew the best way to clean it . . ." she said.

She snapped her fingers, and *Tillie's Tips* appeared.

"My book!" exclaimed Kale.

"Sorry about the switcheroo on the train," Magique whispered. "I wanted you to have a fully magical experience today."

"That's okay," said Kale, remembering all her dreams with another shudder. "I've had enough of cleaning, anyway. For a little while, at least."

"All right, then," said Magique. She snapped her fingers again, and the book was gone. "It's now in the book drop at the Port Innastorm Library."

"Thanks!" said Kale. She reached into her backpack, took out *Professor Magic's Rules of Illusion*, and handed it to Magique.

"No, you keep it," the magician said. "It's the least I can do, to thank you for all your help."

Albertine helped the Bland Sisters into the cabinet as Magique addressed the audience.

"Now, watch as these two are transported to *another world!*" she said. Then she drew the Bland Sisters close and whispered, "Remember, don't ever tell anyone how my cabinet works. You two are magician's assistants for life now, so you're sworn to uphold the Oath. Agreed?"

"Agreed," said Jaundice and Kale.

"Be sure to tell your parents I said thanks, whenever you see them again," Magique said. "I really owe them for sending you along—I can't think of a better way to get to know my nieces."

"Wait," said Jaundice. "So you really are Aunt Shallot?"

"I told you 'Shallot' sounded fuddy-duddy," she reminded them. "I left that name behind long ago. I only answer to Magique now. At some point, we all have to embrace who we really are!"

"That's true," said Jaundice.

"We've always embraced our Blandness. That's who we are," Kale said. "Isn't it?"

Their aunt laughed. "If there's one thing I hope you've learned, it's that nothing is as it seems," she said. And then she closed the cabinet doors.

Inside, it was dark and stuffy. For a few moments, Jaundice and Kale heard murmuring outside, and swelling music . . . and then, they heard nothing.

"It seems so quiet out there," said Kale.

"Almost too quiet. Do you think that's our cue to get out?" said Jaundice. Slowly, she opened the door.

"Where is Magique—I mean, Aunt Shallot?" asked Kale, looking around. "I wish we had time to get to know her, as our aunt, and not as a great detective, or even a great magician. I have so many questions."

"Me, too," said Jaundice. "For instance, where are we?"

The Bland Sisters looked around. Somehow, they emerged

not from the disappearing cabinet, but from a storage locker
at the Dullsville Train Station.

"Whoa. Now *that's* magic," said Kale.

"Shall we go home?" asked Jaundice.

"Yes, let's," said Kale. "I've had enough of mysteries and
magic."

"I suppose you're right." Jaundice said. "Though, speaking

of magic, it was nice to see Magique and Albertine onstage together. They seemed so happy."

"Well, they both love magic. They have that in common. We're not like *our* family *at all*," Kale noted.

"True," Jaundice admitted.

As the Bland Sisters started walking, Jaundice reached into her smock pocket, pulled out the remaining length of string, and began tying a series of complicated knots. Kale reviewed her notes of the day's observations. They really were quite thorough.

As she read, she couldn't help twirling her pen.

When something goes wrong during your act, keep going.
You will probably be the only one to notice.

Chapter Twenty

W hen the Bland Sisters saw their house again at last, it was not the relief they hoped it would be. Right away, they could tell something was wrong.

"Something is wrong," Jaundice said, as they walked up the driveway.

"I'd say more than one thing is wrong," said Kale.

The front door was off its hinges, the furniture was upturned, and the Bland Sisters' lone ficus had been uprooted. Someone had torn up the couch cushions and scattered the stuffing. Even their beloved sock-darning basket

was destroyed, and the socks, thread, needles, and scissors were strewn all over the floor.

"Our customers are not going to be happy about this," Jaundice noted.

As she picked up the pieces of their broken darning egg, Kale sniffed the air.

"What's that . . . smell?" she asked.

Jaundice sniffed, too.

"I didn't take out the trash before we left," Kale said, grimacing. "Serves me right, for forgetting one of *Tillie's Tips*."

Upstairs wasn't as smelly, but the mess was even worse; the mattress was torn open with its springs hanging out, the suitcases were unzipped and the clothes inside torn to shreds, all of the boxes of books and papers and maps were toppled, and the chest containing the Bland Sisters' parents' travel souvenirs had been thrown open, the contents tossed and broken everywhere.

"All of their things," Jaundice whispered. The Bland Sisters kneeled on the floor, their parents' broken mementos and belongings all around them. Kale picked up what was left of one of their parents' pillows. She gave it a good long sniff.

"Who would do this to them. And to us?" she said, handing the tattered pillow to Jaundice, who sniffed, too.

The Bland Sisters put their hands over their hearts.

"There's that ache again," said Jaundice. "It hurts, but it's also kind of nice."

"And it always seems to happen when we're really thinking about our parents," Kale noted.

"Do you think it means we might really . . . *miss* them?" Jaundice wondered.

The Bland Sisters blinked at each other.

"Whoa," said Kale.

"I know," said Jaundice. "We just solved another mystery. About ourselves."

"Maybe it's true, what our parents said in my dream," said Kale. "Maybe we did pack them away. I mean, we did pack all their things away."

"And we packed away how we felt about them, too. Until

now," Jaundice said. "I bet that's why I keep dreaming about that phone that keeps ringing and ringing. It's kind of nice that they keep reaching out to us."

"Even if it is by sending us on adventures against our will," Kale said. She looked around. "Oh, what a mess everything is. It's going to take forever to clean up." It was a dream come true for her, literally. Though, unlike in her dream, their parents weren't trapped at the bottom of the debris.

"It sounds like someone is already vacuuming," said Jaundice.

"If they are, that's a really big vacuum," said Kale. "And it's coming from outside."

The Bland Sisters went downstairs and opened the front door. An airplane could be seen circling overhead.

"I'm having a Feeling," said Kale.

Just then, Miss Penny Post rode up on her bicycle.

"Good morning, ladies!" she said, reaching into her satchel and pulling out a letter. "This just came via Express."

"So did we," said Jaundice. "In a way."

Kale took the envelope from Miss Post and looked at it. "It's from our parents."

With Jaundice looking over her shoulder, Kale opened the envelope and began reading. The handwriting looked even messier than usual, as if it had been written in a hurry.

Darlings,

We hope you enjoyed your time with Aunt Shallot (who, as you've now learned, goes by Magique), and we hope you're not too mad at us for luring you into another adventure. Your father never really shared his sister's (or his father's) interest in magic, so we're glad she could share it with you!

We don't have much time to write, as we have to run—literally. We're being chased by a certain someone we've been hiding from for years, and we have a feeling he might know about you two now, and where to find you. He's just a little bit upset about the scarabs we stole from him (which weren't really his to begin with, by the way), and he'll do anything to get them back. But don't worry—help is on the way! We've sent word to a good friend to come for you. We trust she'll take you under her wing—or "wings," to be more precise!

Looking forward to being reunited, and safe, soon!

Yours, from an undisclosed location,

Your parents

"I suppose we did enjoy our time with Aunt Shallot, even if we didn't know she was Aunt Shallot at the time," Kale admitted. "Among other things, we learned to use our brains, to be observant and quick-thinking, and that we don't like fluffernutters. Still, I'm glad to be home, even if it doesn't look much like home now. Aren't you, sister?"

But Jaundice wasn't listening. Instead, she was reading something scrawled on the other side of the paper.

P.S. One of the scarabs should be on the desk in our study; we've just retrieved its twin. PLEASE put it close to your head at night—ideally, under your pillow. It allows us to talk with you in your dreams. (We'll explain later.)

"Um . . . what does *that* mean?" asked Kale.

Jaundice fished around in one of her smock pockets.

"I know we haven't read our dictionary in a while," she said. "But isn't a scarab a kind of . . . beetle?"

She pulled out the beetle paperweight she'd been carrying around.

"Uh-oh," said Kale.

"All this time, our parents really *were* calling us," Jaundice said.

There, on their front lawn, the airplane was now landing. Books and papers and maps from inside the house had tumbled out with Jaundice and Kale and were now blowing all over the lawn. Kale opened her backpack and scrambled to collect the ephemera, but to no avail. Her copy of *Professor Magic's Rules of Illusion* fell out and was swept away, too.

"Farewell, Professor Magic!" she cried. "I'm sorry we didn't get to know each other better—especially now that I know you were probably my grandfather!"

The pilot of the plane soon slid her window open and shouted, "Your parents sent me! Get in!"

The Bland Sisters looked at each other.

"Are you talking to us?" Jaundice asked.

"Who else would I be talking to?" the pilot shouted. "Come on! We've no time to lose!"

The plane was bright blue, with a bird painted on its side, along with the word BLUEBIRD. The *B* was particularly prominent.

Jaundice gasped.

"'*Plan B*,'" she whispered.

"I'm not really up for another adventure," Kale admitted.

"Me, neither," said Jaundice.

The Bland Sisters sighed.

Jaundice looked back at what remained of their once-cozy, once-safe home, and at all its contents destroyed or lost to

the wind. She looked at the plane, and at the pilot waving frantically. Then she grabbed her sister's hand.

"Hold on tight. Things are about to get interesting," said Jaundice.

"I know," said Kale. "That's what I'm afraid of."

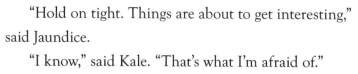

████████████ ACKNOWLEDGMENTS ████████████

M any thanks to everyone who continues to ride this
train with me, particularly Barry Goldblatt, agent and
creative conductor; the talented cherubs at Abrams/Amulet;
Tamar Brazis, Queen of Magic; Jen Hill, the Fluff-O to my
peanut butter; critique partners Anika Denise and Jamie
Michalak, who always keep my writing—and my sanity!—on
track; Rob McDonald, who wanted to be in one of my books
(you're welcome); and Scott and Camden Bowers, my favorite
traveling companions.

ABOUT THE AUTHOR

Kara LaReau was born and raised in Connecticut. She received her master's in fine arts in writing, literature, and publishing from Emerson College in Boston, Massachusetts, and later worked as an editor at Candlewick Press and at Scholastic Press. She is the author of *The Unintentional Adventures of the Bland Sisters: The Jolly Regina*, illustrated by Jen Hill; *Ugly Fish*: and *Otto: The Boy Who Loved Cars*, illustrated by Scott Magoon; and The Infamous Ratsos series, illustrated by Matt Myers. Kara lives in Providence, Rhode Island, with her husband and son.

⊞⊞⊞⊞⊞⊞⊞⊞⊞ ABOUT THE ARTIST ⊞⊞⊞⊞⊞⊞⊞⊞⊞

Jen Hill is the illustrator of *The Unintentional Adventures of the Bland Sisters: The Jolly Regina* by Kara LaReau; *Diana's White House Garden* by Elisa Carbone; and *Doing Her Bit: A Story About the Woman's Land Army of America* by Erin Hagar. She is also the author and illustrator of *Percy and TumTum: A Tale of Two Dogs*. Jen is a graduate from the Rhode Island School of Design, where she studied children's book illustration with David Macaulay and Judy Sue Goodwin Sturges. She lives in Brooklyn, New York, with her husband and her intern, Little Bee, who is very helpful for a cat.